In the Place
Where We Thought We Stood

Peter Nash

Fomite
Burlington, VT

ISBN-13: 978-1-959984-07-8
Library of Congress Control Number: 2023933620

Fomite
58 Peru Street
Burlington, VT 05401
www.fomitepress.com

10/08/2023

For Annie, Ezra, and Isaiah

For Ivan

All night someone holds back,

then crosses the circle of bitter light.

~Alejandra Pizarnik

Jaz in ti. In ti in jaz.

~Ingeborg Bachmann

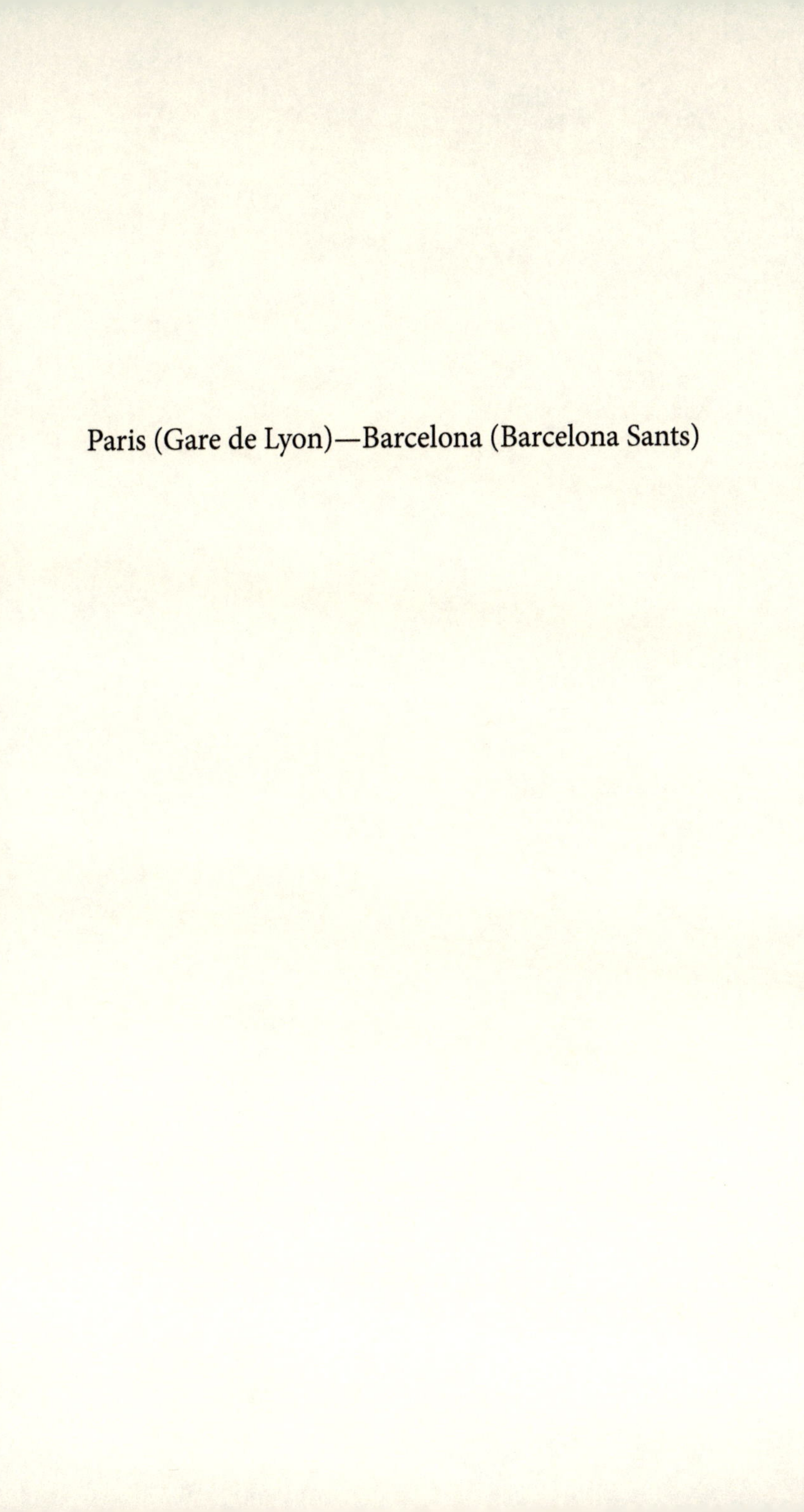

Paris (Gare de Lyon)—Barcelona (Barcelona Sants)

Bachmann.

She tapped the cover of my book. German, eh? No? Well good. I like the Austrians better. The train had yet to leave the station, the Gare de Lyon, and the woman seated beside me was momentarily distracted by a commotion on the platform outside, a man waving his arms, a woman embracing a child. Inside the train it was hot and crowded. I checked the time, adjusted the vent above my seat, and was about to remove my jacket when the woman seated beside me tapped my book again, an old Suhrkamp edition of the novel *Malina* by Ingeborg Bachmann. Hand flat on the cover, she murmured, Such darkness there— the people, the history. Even the language is dark. I used to hate it, the way it twisted my husband's mouth. He was from Dresden, Karl, fell into the tracks here one day, in this very station, crushed to death by a train from Dijon. The remark surprised me, its frankness, its dispassion, and I was about to say something, something conventional, when she patted my knee. Thank you, dear, but no, it wasn't like that. It seems I hardly knew him at all: he hunted, he gambled, he had a mistress in Villejuif. Yet that's a man for you. A German anyhow. Crude, arrogant, selfish to the bone. Take that guy out there, she said, indicating the man on the platform outside. A real pig by the look of him. Used to getting his way, I think. Pork chops, whiskey. Just look at that neck, those jowls. Look at how he waves his arms about him. Not that his wife is an angel, with those rings, that hair. I can imagine her poisoning his coffee one day. What else can she do? She must. What choice does she have? I smiled, shrugged my shoulders. I was on my way to Madrid to sit with my mother-in-law who'd recently suffered a stroke. Apparently she'd asked for me, perhaps thinking I was still there, in her apartment, that I'd not yet returned to Paris, perhaps thinking that her daughter, my wife, was not dead. Yet Teresa was dead; we'd buried her last month, in a vault in La Almudena, though she'd made me swear she'd never be buried, that she'd never have a plaque at her head. I'd promised her that—over sushi one night, by the tomb of Marie Antoinette, and in the gloomy archives of Maisons Victor Hugo, into which we'd happened one day to escape the driving rain. I remembered the scent of her hair that day, a damp, musky smell that had made me think of roots and tubers and dark brown earth. There in the archives of

Maisons Victor Hugo I'd sworn to all the gods she'd named that I'd scatter her ashes by the sea or by a river or in a wood while it was raining. She'd said it was the least I could do. I was thinking of Victor Hugo, of his poem 'The Eruption of Vesuvius', which I'd read for a teacher at school, when the woman seated beside me said, It's funny. I can imagine my daughter doing that, poisoning her husband one day, though she's not even married. Not yet. She lives in Barcelona, in Raval. That's where I'm off to now, she informed me proudly, removing her jacket and filling the air with the scent of gardenias. The man on the platform outside had removed his jacket as well, revealing a number of large, bruise-like tattoos. He was cursing the woman with the child, his fists clenched, his neck strained, his mouth so contorted I was certain he'd strike her, right there before his child, but he didn't. Instead he shuddered strangely, threw his arms in the air. It reminded me of a film I'd seen at the Thalia, some years ago, a murky black and white film from the '50's in which a man strikes a woman in the face where they are standing on an empty railway platform in some war-torn city in Spain. The name of the film was on the tip of my tongue (I could nearly see the words on the poster out front), when the woman seated beside me said, She hates the place, my daughter. Complains about it all the time, the traffic, the noise. Says the people there are rude to her, though she's always been that way, the glass half empty, her toothbrush too soft or too stiff. She complains about everything, poor girl, though mostly she complains about me, calls me a terrible mother, impatient, neglectful, then hangs up the phone. Naturally I forgive her, I forgive her everything, which only makes her angrier. You see, she wants me to yell and scream, to call her selfish and hateful, to tell her I wish she'd never been born. She'd like that, I think, to hear me say such things, but only if she was certain I didn't mean them. Surely she'd prefer it if I didn't mean such things, though to hear them might be good for her, she thinks, *medicinal.* Yet what she'd really like is to know what I think of Hakim, her fiancé, whom I've only met but once, in a crowded Uzbek restaurant in Queens. She'd like to know what I think of him and his crooked little teeth, though he scarcely said a thing, poor man, only blinked his dark eyes and grinned. Certainly I could never tell her what I think of him; she'd hate me forever. She'd say it's because he's Moroccan, a Muslim, but it isn't that, not really. I mean, I hardly know the man. All she's really ever told me about him is that he studied computers in Valencia and that his mother, a widow, lives alone in Tetouan. Which is why I keep my mouth shut. About him anyway, though about other things I'm happy to speak my mind. She doesn't

4

have to listen. She can tell me to stop, she can hang up the phone. And she does, believe me! She's not shy, she's never been shy with me, though I know how she struggles to assert herself with others, to put her best foot forward, her best foot down. She blames me for that, too, says I discouraged her when she was young. She likes to say such things, that I was never around when she needed me, always traveling, always busy with my work. She doesn't intend to be cruel. She says she just can't help it when she knows I'll forgive her before she's even finished shouting. And she's right: I will, I *must*. What else is a mother to do? Yet she's older now, and about to be married. Things are bound to be different, right? It was only when the last of the passengers were settled in their seats and the train had begun to move that she spoke again, if more slowly now, as if in anticipation of the journey ahead. She adjusted her skirt, checked the time on her watch, then folded and refolded the newspaper she'd brought along for the trip, the early edition of *Le Monde*, which I'd read with my coffee this morning, finally stowing it in the pouch on the back of the seat in front of her. For a moment she closed her eyes, I thought she might sleep, when in a whisper, she said, She hates my work, my daughter. She's never understood how I can spend so much time in archives and libraries, tracking down the provenance of this or that old painting, of this or that old necklace or rug. She says it's morbid, that I should let sleeping dogs lie. Of course, the 'dogs' aren't sleeping at all; they're dead, murdered. The Jews, I mean. Murdered by the millions, which certainly she knows. She'd just rather not think about it. After all, she's young and still pretty. She's convinced I've wasted my talents as a lawyer, that I've frittered away my career, my life, though she really doesn't understand my work these days, for I have nothing to do with the provenance of things. Not anymore. Now I spend my time tracking down people instead—a sort of genealogist in reverse! You see, once the ownership of an item has been established, it's my task to discover if there are any descendants still living to claim it. I've told her that, that I've got the good part of the job. I knock on a door, I introduce myself, and the woman standing there usually breaks down and cries. Unless it's a man. Men don't cry, not usually, they tend to scowl at me, at the thought of what I've brought them: some candlesticks, a gaudy Meissen clock, an inscribed, leather-bound edition of the songs and poems of Heinrich Heine. Why, I've knocked on doors all over the world, in Rio, Cape Town, and Beirut. Last week I knocked on a door in Dhaka, where I listened to an Irishman, fluent in Bengali, selling computers on the phone. That's what my daughter doesn't understand, the people part. It's what keeps me going, the look on their faces, the stories they tell, though sometimes they're disappointed, it's true, or simply frightened, they look at me aghast, as if afraid even to *see* what the past has unearthed for them: a Biedermeier brooch, some old letters, a pair of Chinese teacups—even a battered old mohel's kit, complete with knife, shields, and scissors! It was to a fat young man in Pittsburg that I handed that! Naturally they must sign for the objects; there are forms to complete. Still, it's generally pleasant work. They're often reluctant to see me go. I nodded, I smiled. It was the most I could do, for I'd spent a restless night thinking about my mother-in-law, and about the train ride to Madrid, where there'd be no one at the station to meet me. I was in no mood to travel, to be somewhere else. For weeks I'd been sitting at my favorite café, at the same small table, I'd lost track of the brandies, the days, sometimes reading, sometimes writing, sometimes merely drowsing like a cat in the sun, for the clouds had finally scattered, the sky a wan and aimless blue. Overnight young couples had appeared, fashions had changed, I'd heard music in the streets. Even when it had rained, as it had some days, when the cars had hissed by and the plane trees had turned silvery in the light, there'd been a lushness to the sound, the scent, a promise in the air that had made me think I'd return to New York, after all, to my apartment in Brooklyn, as I'd promised my sister I would. The problem was Teresa's things. This morning I'd found the silver necklace I'd bought for her in Taxco, with its old-fashioned clasp, the pearl-sized balls still cool to the touch and tarnished nearly black, for she'd refused to polish them. She'd felt that silver, like people, should age. Then there were her books and her photographs, which she'd framed by the dozens for our walls. And there were her shoes, too, perhaps the saddest of what remained of her. Some days I studied the heels of them, the scuff marks, the cracks; in one pair, a pair of summer flats, I'd found the slender imprint of her feet. Restless now I checked my phone. I was due to hear back from my friend, Antoine, who was to have returned from Senegal yesterday, a place—with its markets and sunshine and brightly colored boats—that suddenly seemed fantastical to me. I pictured his burnished skin, his fine white teeth. I imagined the stories he would tell. And not for the first time I wondered why he ever came back. All across Paris it was raining, a steady, miserable rain. There was little to see, to believe in. It was as if for years I'd been sleeping and only now had begun to dream. And what a dream—graffiti, trash, and the ugly twilight sprawl of office parks, housing projects, and belching petrochemical plants that never failed to bewilder me. I knew the route well: Valence, Nîmes,

Montpellier, Narbonne, Perpignan, Girona, then on to Barcelona, to Barcelona Sants, where, after a sandwich and coffee, I'd catch the next train to Madrid. I didn't want to go there, not again. I didn't want to see María Pascuala, to touch her hand, to hear her voice. I didn't want to set foot in her darkly shuttered room, with its saints and angels, its reeking candles, its gilt-framed portrait of El Caudillo by her bed. I didn't want to sit alone in her kitchen, to eat her food and drink her wine, to chat with her housekeeper, Andolça Mira, a skulking, pious old woman who didn't like me and mumbled her words. I didn't want to repeat it, any of it, to walk the same dull steps, to say the same dull things, to feel the same dull sadness I'd felt. Irritably now I removed my jacket, inserted my earbuds, and was search-ing the music on my phone for the raga I'd been listening to this morning, when I realized that the woman seated beside me was still talking, telling me something about a pair of drawings by Bonnard, two studies from a sketch-book he'd kept in Le Cannet. She was telling me about having recently restored them to a descendant of the orig-inal owner, to a woman, a doctor, in Prague. That's the funny thing, she said, Hitler hated his work. His paintings anyway. Apparently their colors made him shriek! It was a remark that pleased her, I sensed she'd made it before, in some other setting, on some other train, and for the first time I considered her, my fellow passenger, her coppery brown hair, her lightly powdered cheeks, her stylish if matronly clothes. I studied her fingernails, with their clear matte polish, the fine gold bangles at her wrists. Teresa would have liked her, I thought, she would have liked the way she talked, the way, like women of a certain age, she said what she pleased and at length. Look, she cried now, pressing her shoulder to mine, I have the drawings right here on my phone! Removing my glasses, I squinted at the tiny screen—a few trees by water, a young woman asleep. Striking, aren't they? she said. Just a few deft strokes. I agreed, they were lovely. Especially the one of the woman dreaming. It seemed I'd never slept that way. Outside the light flickered; I saw a stand of poplars, an empty ambulance by the side of the road. I'd always liked traveling by train, the sense of timelessness, of time suspended, of being somewhere and nowhere at once. The train had picked up speed; we passed a cement factory, some wastewater ponds, then a half dozen fuel tanks on one of which had been painted a large, bloodshot eye. I considered getting out my laptop to do some work, if only to make a schedule for my days in Madrid, but I hadn't the mind for it, any of it, and closed my eyes, soothed by the gentle rocking of the train and by the raga playing softly in my ears, when, apparently having missed the transition, I heard the woman seated beside me say, It's true, I feel for lovers these days, the way they thrash about. My Ellie can hardly think straight, for all the fretting she does. I mean, when does a person just *live*? All the worrying, all the make-up and talk shows and magazines. And for what? It makes me wonder if love is even possible anymore, the kind that just happens, feels right. Tired as I was, I was happy to listen to her, as she required little reciprocation from me. Instead I gazed out the window, distracted, diverted, by the dreary parade of office blocks and ware-houses, and by the sudden green blur of embankments and trees. It was April and I'd hardly begun my translation of the collected correspondence of Ingeborg Bachmann and the poet Paul Celan, though I'd signed a contract for it over two years ago, and just last week had promised my editor he'd have a draft of it by the end of July. In fact I had begun it: I'd been working on it ever since graduate school, when I'd made my first attempts to render their letters and telegrams in English. Since then I'd written numerous arti-cles about them and their relationship, and about her, her writing, her life. I'd given papers, had sat on panels, and had translated a number of her lesser known works, including her war diary, three of her radio plays, and an early volume of her poetry called *The Deferred Time* or *Die gestundete Zeit*. I'd even taught a course on her fiction at

NYU. Now I pictured the files in the rack above my seat. God knows why I'd brought them. I knew that once in Madrid I'd never even look at them. Such was the effect of the city on me. I'd drink too much, sleep late, then wander the streets of Retiro until I craved another gin. And soon I'd hate myself again. I'd go jogging, I'd visit the Prado, I'd buy a Spanish newspaper and try to read it in the park, knowing all the while that Andolça Mira would find me there, she always did, sidling up beside me in her blunt, misshapen shoes, so that I'd have no choice but to follow her back to the apartment, to María Pascuala, to sit like a nurse at her side. The building itself unnerved me. Arriving by taxi or on foot, I couldn't bear to consider it, the dark, wrought-iron balconies, the heavily draped windows, for fear I'd look up at the roof from which Teresa had jumped. I hated everything about the place—the doormen, the lobby, the bright padded hallways with their ghastly trompe l'oeil. And I hated the smell of it, a sickening compound of lilies, detergents, and wax. Designed in the Belle Epoque style by the Catalan architect, Eduard Ferrés i Puig, the building filled me now—even the thought of it—with an extravagant and intractable dread. Officially, Teresa had died in a car accident, struck from behind by a truck hauling bricks, a story I'd rehearsed so many times, for the sake of her mother, I sometimes found myself believing it. Just yesterday I'd repeated it to one of the waiters at my favorite café, even elaborating upon the details for him—the rain, the traffic, the small crumpled car. Encouraged by his reaction (he'd actually seemed tempted to sit with me), I'd told him she'd just had her hair done, that the car had been filled with groceries. What's more, I'd told him that the driver of the truck had been drunk at the time, that he was a gangster, a smuggler, a Turk, though I'd quickly recanted the last part (for my waiter himself had looked Turkish), adding bluffly that Spaniards were simply like that, they called everyone Turks. In fact I knew little about Spaniards. Even less about Turks. Teresa was the only Spaniard I'd ever really known, a person who every day seemed less familiar to me. Indeed it was an effort now to recall even the simplest things about her—the sound of her voice, her laughter, the feel of her lips on my cheek. Her books and clothes, her lotions and perfumes, not even the photographs of her (of which I had dozens on my laptop and phone) were enough to make her real to me, to quicken the millions of tiny impulses by which she'd lived as a person in my brain. In every photograph she looked dead to me, dead already, as if even then she'd known, as if even then she'd been biding her time, so that nothing was the same to me; all I remembered seemed changed. Once more I adjusted the vent above my seat. The air in the car was stifling and I pressed my forehead against the window, cool and blurry with rain. It always surprised me, the suddenness with which the city gave way to farmland, to dark green fields stretching as far as the eye could see. Here and there the forest reasserted itself, a stone house appeared, a patch of vineyard, when, with what seemed a mythical stealth, there rose a tall white turbine, its great white blades turning slowly in the air. One day, just a few days after I'd returned from Madrid, I'd lost my way home from my favorite café. It was raining hard, the streets were empty, my shoes and socks were wet. Cold, confused, I followed one street after another, peering into shops and restaurants without recognizing a person, a thing. At one point I heard sirens, when a face appeared—wretched and moonlike—in a window just above me. It took me more than an hour to find my way back to my building that night, to recognize my corner, my block, so that I had to fumble in the darkness for my keys. Not even the next morning had the rain let up, the clouds so dark, so low upon the city, I had to switch on the lights to get dressed. I remembered that my neighbor was singing that day, an aria from *Tosca* or *Lucia di Lammermoor*—I'm never sure which, as she's rehearsing for both. She told me so herself one day, when I met her on the stairs, a woman half my age with weak, doleful eyes and a wryly twisted lip. She told me she was Hungarian, a Croat from Pécs, that her mother and father were dead. That morning I'd listened to her singing, heard her singing all day, as I staggered through the hours, folding laundry, paying bills, and trying against all odds to get back to my work. The last letter I'd translated was a short one from Celan to Bachmann, dated 23 November, 1957. I'd numbered it 63. Sent to Bachmann from Paris, from his address on rue de Longchamp, where he was living with his wife, Gisèle Lestrange, Celan had written it not long after the resumption of their affair. I'd read it over coffee this morning and despaired:

> Just one line, to thank you, with all my heart,
> for everything.
> To think that we had to hound our
> hearts to death in the past over such trifles,
> Ingeborg! Whom were we obeying, tell me,
> whom?
> But now I am coming soon, not for long;
> for one day, for another—if you want and
> allow me to.
> Let us then go in search of the lamp,
> Ingeborg, you and I, us.
>
> Paul

It wasn't so much my translation of it that bothered me, but the fact that, at some point, I'd lost the thread of their thinking, the sense of what he'd meant. Since Teresa's death, I'd struggled to conjure their voices, to get inside their heads. I remembered how Teresa had loved their telegrams and letters. Some nights, as we'd lain together in bed, she'd had me read them aloud to her, as she listened to the rain or to the traffic on the avenue below. I'd read them aloud to her, often dozens in a row, first in German, then in English or French, filling in the gaps as I could, when inevitably she'd asked me about my mother. At first I'd restricted myself to sharing only the most banal details about her life, idle tidbits about her work, her friends, her taste for Turkish sweets—trivia, particulars, with which Teresa had quickly grown impatient, demanding, with the obstinacy of a child, that I tell her more, much more, that I relinquish what I knew. Yet something had restrained me, so that night after night I'd told her about everyone *but* my mother, weaving them together—my aunt, my sister, the old cashier from the bistro downstairs—into a woman so odd, so improbable, that Teresa had cursed me in her anguish, her grief. For it had seemed very much like grief to me, what she'd felt, as if she'd lost something dear to her, as if something secret and precious had been taken away. I couldn't have explained my reluctance, I myself didn't understand it, my mother then shameless and dead. It was something about the way Teresa had looked at me on those occasions, a hunger, a greediness in her eyes, that had made me hesitate, draw back. In the story of my mother she'd seemed to sense something she *knew* and *needed*, something I myself couldn't see. Years before, in a fit of soul-searching, my sister, too, had pressed me for details about our mother, a woman she felt she'd never really known. It was about the other woman—the one with whom I'd lived alone, here in Paris, who'd written and lectured and smoked Gauloises Brunes—that she'd been so eager, so desperate, to learn. The summer Colette turned fifteen, my mother and I had left New York for good, had packed our belongings and moved here to Paris, to Batignolles, the neighborhood in which her uncle and cousin still lived. She'd had enough of our father, of his hectoring and abuse, and had decided to return to France, to raise her children here. Yet my sister (no doubt persuaded by my father) had declined to go, choosing to remain in New York with her friends. Time passed; I hardly spoke with Colette. Now and then we exchanged letters, written by hand and filled with the sort of minutiae one relies on when there is nothing else to say. Once or twice a year she flew to Paris to stay with us, we went shopping, ate in restaurants, when she gathered her things and flew home. By the time she was in college she'd come to look a lot like our mother, the way she dressed, the way she cut her hair. I have a photograph of the two of them by the tracks in the métro, and even their smiles are the same. I was thinking of Colette, of sending her the photograph, if I could remember where I put it, when I was startled by an announcement from the conductor, something about a delay in Valence, about some work on the train tracks ahead. The woman beside me was chatting with the man across the aisle, a retired plumber from Arles who was returning home after a week-long visit with his son, a designer of women's handbags. The woman beside me was telling the man about the shop where she'd bought her shoes, the stylish red leather ones she was wearing. They're Italian, I heard her tell him, a remark that clearly pleased him, as his wife, Francesca, was from Rome. I considered getting something to eat from the café-bar, a sandwich or a bag of chips, but hadn't the energy to excuse myself and get up. It had been my plan to pack some food for the trip but I'd lost track of the time this morning, diverted by my work and by a story in the paper about a man from Oran who'd been knifed in the street. For some reason the story had made me think of my mother, though the connection was uncertain, obscure. It often happened, these days, that two things suddenly became linked in my mind, though I struggled in vain to relate them. I'd stub my toe and think of Kant. I'd lick an envelope, see Jaffa, smell fish. As far as

I knew, my mother had never been to Algeria, let alone to Oran. Certainly she'd never been stabbed. Nor had she read the daily papers, she'd hated them, preferring her poetry and novels instead. Once more the connection had escaped me, though I could sense it there, crouched like a gremlin in my brain. I pictured my mother at her desk, heard the clattering of her typewriter, felt my vision and stomach contract. It had been a while since I'd thought of her, at least in any concerted way. I'd gotten used to merely glancing at her, at my memory of her, as one might at a face or figure in the street. In the midst of reading the article in the newspaper this morning, I'd remembered an occasion I couldn't recall having ever remembered before, as if, after years of being tangled in the weeds of my brain, it had finally worked itself free. It was autumn, the air chilly, the sky a streaked if lucent gray. My mother and I were waiting in line for the Ferris wheel at the old Palisades Amusement Park in New Jersey. From there, I could see the Hudson River below us, flat and polished by the light. I remembered my mother was pacing and mumbling and smoking furiously. I remembered her telling me that she needed to get up somewhere high so she could see again, that everything was cloudy in her brain. Gazing out over the rain-slick rooftops this morning, with their broken tiles and old antennae, I'd remembered the scene with a nearly violent clarity—her smoking and pacing and squeezing my arm. I'd remembered the strange, dank smell of her coat. It was a smell I'd later come to associate with our life here in Paris, with the dark feeble days when she'd paced before the drafty old windows of our apartment, smoking and mumbling and chewing her lip. There'd been a restlessness to her, to the way she'd smoked and eaten, to the way she'd talked on the phone. Even while sleeping she'd twisted and turned. At the time, she'd been obsessed with the work of Lucy Dawidowicz, Raul Hilberg, and Hannah Arendt, and with that of the historian and journalist, Gitta Sereny, best known for her study of the Nazi, SS-Hauptsturmführer Franz Stangl. My mother had met her once, at a conference in Graz. Between sessions they'd taken a walk together. She'd told my mother she was pretty. Sereny's work had proven integral to my mother's final book, an exhaustive study of modern evil, which, despite my efforts, was still not in print. Entitled *The Quiet Men: Bureaucratic Murder in the 20th Century*, it represented the culmination of more than twenty years of thinking and research. At its heart was what, since the trial of Adolf Eichmann, were known as *Schreibtischtäter* or "desk killers", those murderous bureaucrats "with white collars and cut fingernails and smooth-shaven cheeks who do not need to raise their voices." I remembered the day she'd finished the book—the flush in her cheeks, the high, bright look in her eyes. And I remembered the way she'd cried. Years before she'd been accused of plagiarizing the work of another French scholar in her study of the collaboration between French women and the Nazis during the German Occupation, which accusation, while ultimately groundless, had nearly destroyed her career, not to mention her spirit, her will. This latest book was to have saved her. Indeed the initial prospects had seemed good. Shortly before my mother killed herself, she'd formed a relationship with an editor at a certain well-known publishing house in Paris. Twice they'd met for lunch, they'd liked each other at once, when the woman had fallen ill and disappeared, so that, for all my mother's efforts to replace her, to renew her connection with the press, her project—so taxing, so painful in its creation—had slipped through the cracks. Yet she'd left me a clue. Not long after her death, I'd discovered amidst her books and papers the name of another editor with whom she'd corresponded, a man named Vernier who'd agreed to talk with her about the project. Having no idea if they'd ever actually met, if even he was still working at the press, I'd written to him at once, and had been surprised to receive a brief, if encouraging reply. Shortly thereafter, he'd asked me to send him the manuscript in full. He'd spent months with it, a whole winter and spring, yet I hadn't heard from him. Not a word. I'd emailed him, called him, left him a message on his phone. When at last he'd contacted me, it was to tell me he'd been promoted, and that he'd passed on the manuscript to one of the junior editors there, a brilliant young woman who specialized in *such things*. Briefly I'd talked with the woman on the phone; we'd laughed a bit; she said she'd be in touch. Then the press had been purchased by another concern. She'd told me we'd have to wait and see. More than a year has passed since then, and I've still not managed to get a contract from her, to convince her to publish the work. That and more was troubling me this morning when I arrived at the station. I'd woken early, in a haze of anxiety and confusion, to find it still dark out, still raining, so that I'd wanted nothing more than to return to my apartment, close the blinds, and sleep for days. All my reasons for living—for rising in the morning, for working each day, for getting on this train—had vanished in a wink, so that surely I'd have drunk myself to death had it not been for the simple habit of living, for the tug of the world at my strings. That I cooked, that I paid my bills, that I washed and folded my clothes, seemed nothing short of miraculous to me. Some mornings I caught myself shaving: I stared at the man in the mirror, at his pale skin and dark-ringed eyes, at his thinning brown hair, amazed at the gentle way he worked the razor on his chin. I saw him making coffee, making toast. I studied his hands, nimble hands, as they buttoned his buttons and tied the laces of his boots and sneakers and shoes. And each day I watched him as he stepped out the door. I was alive, after all. Shopkeepers greeted me, we chatted easily, they handed me my change. One evening, while out walking, I collided with a cyclist who cursed me roundly in Dutch. Yet always the reprieve was brief, for there were days, many days, when I didn't leave the apartment at all, hardly stirring from my bed. I dozed, I murmured, I counted wildly, strangely, my mind a blur of scores and tallies and codes. It was from there, from beneath the blankets each morning, that I pieced together the world. It always started with the pipes, with their matinal gurgling in the wall by my head. I heard footsteps above me, the flushing of a toilet, then the plangent rush of water in a shower or tub. Alone, as if alerted by some new intuition, I saw things I'd never seen before, heard sounds I'd never heard—a clicking and clanking, a beeping of signals, the dark, metal trilling of insects and birds. I considered the shape of the room, an ugly little room with an ugly little spirit that had taunted me since the day I'd moved in. Drunk once, I'd told Teresa about it; she'd laughed at me; I remembered her eyebrows, her teeth. A spirit? she'd cried. That spirit—Eugenius—is me! I'd been so in love with her, when we met, that I hadn't thought twice about the dingy five flights to her door. The taps leaked, the walls were cracked, the windows sealed shut with old paint. And the views? The views left me chary and blind. This morning, I'd woken feeling especially out of sorts, my eyes burning, my jaw aching, so that it had taken me longer than usual to pack up my things. Along with my clothes, and with the various items I needed for my work, I'd included the final draft of my mother's manuscript in its battered plastic cover. Last spring was the first time I'd had the nerve to consider it, even to read the dedication. Of course, she'd dedicated the book to me, to my sister and me: *Ce livre est à vous*. More than eight hundred pages long, it had taken me months to finally finish it. Certain sections had left me speechless, others bitter, exhausted, or numb. Her voice rarely faltered, her reasoning—the accretion of facts and figures— so relentless, so exacting, that at points in my reading I'd gasped. The book's epigraph alone had haunted me for weeks, a Nazi memorandum from one Security Police officer, Willy Just, to his superior, SS-Obersturmbannführer Walter Rauf, in which he describes the adjustments he is considering for the "Spezialwagen" or mobile gas chambers with which the Nazis were experimenting at the time:

> II D 3 a (9) NI. 214/42 G.RS.
> Berlin, 5 June 1942
> Only copy.
> Top Secret!

I. Note:

Conc.: Technical adjustments to special vans at present in service and to those that are in production.

Since December 1941, ninety-seven thousand have been processed, using three vans, without any defects showing up in the vehicles. The explosion that we know took place at Kulmhof is to be considered an isolated case. The cause can be attributed to improper operation. In order to avoid such incidents, special instructions have been addressed to the services concerned. Safety has been increased considerably as a result of these instructions.

Previous experience has shown that the following adjustments would be useful:

1.) In order to facilitate the rapid distribution of CO, as well as to avoid a buildup of pressure, two slots, ten by one centimeters, will be bored at the top of the rear wall. The excess pressure would be controlled by an easily adjustable hinged metal valve on the outside of the vents.

2.) The normal capacity of the vans is nine to ten per square meter [= 10.8 sq. ft.]. The capacity of the larger special Saurer vans is not so great. The problem is not one of overloading but of off-road maneuverability on all terrains, which is severely diminished in this van. It would appear that a reduction in the cargo area is necessary. This can be achieved by shortening the compartment by about one meter. The problem cannot be solved by merely reducing the number of subjects treated, as has been done so far. For in this case a longer running time is required, as the empty space also needs to be filled with CO. On the contrary, were the cargo area smaller, but fully occupied, the operation would take considerably less time, because there would be no empty space.

3.) The pipe that connects the exhaust to the van tends to rust, because it is eaten away from the inside by liquids that flow into it. To avoid this the nozzle should be so arranged as to point downward. The liquids will thus be prevented from flowing into [the pipe].

4.) To facilitate the cleaning of the vehicle, an opening will be made in the floor to allow for drainage. It will be closed by a watertight cover about twenty to thirty centimeters in diameter, fitted with an elbow siphon that will allow for the drainage of thin liquids. The upper part of the elbow pipe will be fitted with a sieve to avoid obstruction. Thicker dirt can be removed through the large drainage hole when the vehicle is cleaned. The floor of the vehicle can be tipped slightly. In this way all the liquids can be made to flow toward the center and be prevented from entering the pipes.

5.) The observation windows that have been installed up to now could be eliminated, as they are hardly ever used. Considerable time will be saved in the production of the new vans by avoiding the difficult fitting of the window and its airtight lock.

6.) Greater protection is needed for the lighting system. The grille should cover the lamps high enough up to make it impossible to break the bulb. It seems that these lamps are hardly ever turned on, so the users have suggested that they could be done away with. Experience shows, however, that when the back door is closed and it gets dark inside, the load pushes hard against the door. The reason for this is that when it becomes dark inside the load rushes toward what little light remains. This hampers the locking of the door. It has also been noticed that the noise provoked by the locking of the door is linked to the fear aroused by the darkness. It is therefore expedient to keep the lights on before the operation and during the first few minutes of its duration. Lighting is also useful for night work and for the cleaning of the interior of the van.

7.) To facilitate the rapid unloading of the vehicles, a removable grid is to be placed on the floor. It will slide on rollers on a U-shaped rail. It will be removed and put in position by means of a small winch placed under the vehicle. The firm charged with the alterations has stated that it is not able to continue for the moment, due to a lack of staff and materials. Another firm will have to be found.

The technical changes planned for the vehicles already in operation will be carried out when and as major repairs to these vehicles prove necessary. The alterations in the ten Saurer vehicles already ordered will be carried out as far as possible. The manufacturer made it clear in a meeting that structural alterations, with the exception of minor ones, cannot be carried out for the moment. An attempt must therefore be made to find another firm that can carry out, on at least one of these ten vehicles, the alterations and adjustments that experience has proved to be necessary. I suggest that the firm in Hohenmauth be charged with the execution. Due to present circumstances, we shall have to expect a later date of completion for this vehicle. It will then not only be kept available as a model but also be used as a reserve vehicle. Once it has been tested, the other vans will be withdrawn from service and will undergo the same alterations.

II. To Gruppenleiter II D SS-Obersturmbannführer Rauff for examination and decision.

I'd found I could only read the book by daylight, when I

was sitting in a park or café, surrounded by people, by life. I'd read a chapter then go for a walk to clear my head. Sometimes only brandy would do. Yet each day I'd read on, for amidst the horrors I could sometimes hear my mother's voice. It was like a secret understanding I'd had with her, a glimpse of the frailty behind it all, the pain and anguish, the fear and trembling that had finally over-whelmed her. As a child I'd rarely known what she was thinking, though her work had colored every aspect of my life. Each night as I'd fallen asleep, I'd listened to her typing, to the fearsome clatter of the keys, heard her coughing and pacing, when often in the morning she'd be gone. I remem-bered her room—the desk by the door, the green-speckled curtains, the stylish Danish armchair in which she used to read to me at night, a wooden lounge chair with mus-tard-yellow cushions and a symbol-like scratch on one arm. And I remembered her bed beneath the window there, a simple daybed with a blue velvet bolster on which by day she'd scattered her papers and books. I knew she'd loved me, she'd often told me so, stroking my face and brushing the hair from my eyes. One day I'd find a new book on my desk, one I'd mentioned to her in passing; another day she'd surprise me by taking me for a ham-burger and French fries at a place near Champ de Mars. It was her trips to Berlin that had been the hardest part for me. I'd never complained, at least that I can remember, packing my bag, each time, and walking the long short distance to her uncle's apartment, where he'd lived in a shamble of books and old furnishings with his sullen, housebound wife. In Berlin my mother had usually stayed with friends, people she'd known for years, though for a time I'd imagined she'd had another family there, a German family—a husband and daughter and son. I'd pictured her walking and talking with a boy my age; I'd seen them laughing by a fountain in a park. And for some reason there were always pigeons billing and cooing at their feet. It was only after she'd taken me with her, on one of her many trips there, that my fears had been allayed. Her friends, professors like her, had seemed unremarkable to me. Like her, they'd talked and smoked and paced the airless rooms. I'd seen no children at all, though there'd been a number of lovely parks through which we'd wandered that fall. My mother had hated Berlin, she'd often told me so, the cold and wind, the churlish people, the dirty cobbled sidewalks with their tarnished brass plates (*Here lived Max Bayer... Here lived Sophie Cahn...*), though clearly she'd loved the city, too, the bookshops and galleries, the restaurants, museums, and cafés, returning home each time with a tried, if wistful look. Usually she'd brought me souvenirs, maps and postcards and cloying little sweets in round blue tins, though she'd rarely known what to make of them, the gifts, what to say, rummaging around in her suitcase, each time, as if she'd had no idea what she'd brought me. It was only later, some years after her death, that I'd learned she'd had a lover in Berlin, a man, a painter named Hans. He'd tracked me down in Paris one day, eager to meet me and to give me a box of my mother's things. It was mostly books she'd left with him, though there was also a pair of earrings, a familiar paisley shawl, a few black and white photographs of me, and an old passport of hers, in the densely franked pages of which I'd found her membership card for the Berlin State Library, the Staatsbibliothek or 'Stabi', as she'd liked to call it. He'd been pleasant enough, the painter, we'd spent the day together, walking and talking, and discussing the various exhibits at the Delacroix Museum, a modest, uncrowded place near the Church of Saint Germain de Prés. As the day had happened to be sunny, and not too cold, we'd sat for a while on one of the benches in the little garden there. Perhaps a few years older than my mother would have been, he was a strikingly handsome man who'd insisted on speaking English with me, though by then my German was quite good, even reciting a poem for me, Whitman's 'I Saw in Louisiana a Live-oak Growing'. Over the course of the day he'd shared with me any number of stories about my mother, smoking, chuckling to himself, sometimes brushing his long blond hair from his eyes, stories about her intelligence and beauty, and about her sovereign contempt for the world, what with a wink he'd called *the joy of the very serious*. He'd told me she'd often sung to him in Norwegian, silly folk songs she'd learned as girl, that she'd liked to go skating, that she'd stopped at nothing, some nights, until she'd had her fill of currywurst, French fries, and beer—none of which stories I'd believed, not really, for few of them had rung true to me. For my mother had hated sports, had eaten like bird. What had seemed clear was that he was trying to unravel something, some matter in his brain, to get at something *through me*, a dissemblance, a dishonesty, for which I'd hadn't the conscience to fault him. Sitting there that day, it had never occurred to me that his stories about my mother were true, that she'd been someone else there, in Berlin, someone strange and outlandish to me. One of the stories he'd told me, one I hadn't believed at the time, it had seemed too florid, far-fetched, was about an occasion, just after my mother had arrived there one winter, when she'd called him on the telephone in the early hours of the morning, weeping and shivering and begging him to find her. After a night spent drinking with friends, she'd gotten lost and had not known what to do. She'd left her coat somewhere, it was snowing hard, and she'd cut her lip wide open, she'd had no idea how, certain only that the blood had stained her new shirt. It had made her angry to think she'd stained her new shirt. And he'd told me another story, too, about a time when my mother had been followed by a man through the woods. It had happened in Norway, where she and her parents had spent their summers when she was young. It was there, near the town of Rosendal, where the nights were cool and the dirt was rich and dark, that the man had followed her through the woods. He'd followed her one evening, some-times drawing closer, sometimes falling back, a man with a stick and crumpled felt hat who'd taunted her with shrill and bird-like cries, sounds that had made her feel sick, uneasy, like she was dying inside. There by the Hardangerfjorden, Hans had told me, she'd filled her own mouth with the dirt. It was a story I hadn't heard before, it was not the sort of story she'd have told me, though she'd often spoken of her summers there, in Norway, of the friendly people, the birds and flowers, the ghoulish old plum tree in the yard. Her father, a geologist for a French-Belgian oil concern, had marveled endlessly at the region's fjords, at the thought of the great retreat of glaciers that had made them, while her mother, a music professor at the École Normale Superieure, had paid them little mind at all, renting bicycles for them, stuffing herself with gravlax and pickled herring, and sitting for hours in the small buzzing yard with her cold press paper and watercolor paints. To reciprocate, I'd told Hans everything I knew about her summers there, about the glaciers and fjords, about the gravlax and herring, about the ghoulish old plum tree in the yard. Moved by his reaction, and surprised by the easy, natural forms my mother assumed in my words, I'd told him about her bicycle accident when she was twelve (he must have seen the scar on her hip), about the summer we'd spent in Tel Aviv, and about her childhood obsession with the Panama Canal, an obsession triggered by a book of paintings she'd found one day in the old, ramshackle boathouse in Rosendal, paintings by the Norwegian American artist, Jonas Lie, who'd captured in oils the heroic construction of 'the path between the seas'. Created on site in 1913, the paintings had made a lasting impression on my mother, she'd explained to me, some many years later, when together we'd thumbed through the glossy plates. I remembered she'd made a point of warning me not to confuse the painter, Jonas Lie, with his father's brother-in-law, the author, Jonas Lie, nor certainly with the collaborator, SS-Sturmbannführer Jonas Lie, the Minister of Police and commander of the dreaded Freiwilligen Legion "Norwegen". I'd told Hans all of these things and more, not knowing what he'd heard before, or, if in fact he'd heard them, which versions of them he'd heard, for stories were never fixed and stable, I knew, we told them differently to different people in different times and places. Even the stories of others, the stories they'd told us, were as plastic as putty, once we'd heard them, we shaped them as we pleased. Such and more I'd thought about that day, in the little garden of the Delacroix Museum. I'd thought about the stories Hans had told me, about why he'd told them one way and not another way, included one thing and not another thing, colored one thing and not another thing, and left another thing dark. And I'd thought about the stories I'd told *him*, about the things I'd included and colored, about the things I'd left dark. For I'd shared with him a host of other stories, as well, most if not all of which he'd seemed to have heard before, in some version, some form, though he'd made no effort to stop me, to amend what I'd said, appraising me gently with his pale blue eyes. Spurred by what demons, I cannot say, I'd told him everything I could recall about my mother, speaking madly, deliriously, in a way I hadn't talked about her in years. I'd talked until my eyes were tearing, until my throat was dry, when it had occurred to me, there, where we sat in the little garden of the Delacroix Museum, that all the people I knew, and had ever known, were bound together in exactly that way, by the stories we told, that there was no escaping it, our need, our propensity to talk, to recount our pleasures, our griefs, that finally there was little more to us than the stories we told, that we were put on this earth, each one of us, one here, one there, one rich, one poor, by some helplessly talking Being for no other reason than to talk, one word dragging other words behind it, that we were but talking contraptions, really, weak, soft talking machines that talked and talked, even in our heads we talked, even in our nightmares, our dreams. We couldn't help it, to anyone who'd listen we prattled and prated, we stammered and spluttered, we told them our fortunes, our tales, some of which were true and some of which were not true, or some of which were partly true and partly not-true, or only *semi*-true, for we rarely told our stories to be true. We gabbled and chattered, we babbled and yammered, we preached, we blathered, we *talked*: friends talked, neighbors talked, strangers talked, widows talked, parents talked, children talked, teachers talked, students talked, clowns talked, generals talked, soldiers talked, lovers talked, dreamers talked, writers talked, artists talked, dancers talked, actors talked, cooks talked, waiters talked, maids talked, beggars talked, thieves talked, singers talked, brewers talked, porters talked, nurses talked, doctors talked, dentists talked, clerks talked, judges talked, lawyers talked, farmers talked, gods talked, prophets talked, saints talked, yogis talked, rabbis talked, priests talked, imams talked, nuns talked, bakers talked, barbers talked, heroes talked, cowards talked, hermits talked, tailors talked, plumbers talked, bankers talked, even Nazis talked, they talked and talked and talked. It was in April, 1971, in one of the meeting rooms of the new remand prison in Düsseldorf, a modern block room usually reserved for inmates and their lawyers, a room all but identical to the nearby cell in which the former SS Officer Franz Stangl had spent his days since his capture in Brazil, listening to the radio and thinking about chess, a room with the same barred windows, the same tiled floor, the same dreary view of the paved indoor yard. It was there in that modern block room in the new remand prison in Düsseldorf that the Nazi Franz Stangl had agreed to talk with the historian and journalist, Gitta Sereny. For more than seventy hours running he'd told her all about himself, about his education and career, about his love of the zither, about his abhorrence of fish and tinned meat, for the Nazis had loved to talk, before the war and during the war and especially after the war, when they were in prison or in hiding or living out their days in some drab and cheerless suburb of Frankfurt, Stuttgart, or Bonn, though by then most of them were dead, some hanged, some suicides, some merely dead, deceased, hearts stopped, tongues swollen, limbs cold and blue in their cold and narrow beds. One could fill a thousand notebooks with their stories, these Nazis, men like Eichmann and Göring, like Mengle, Goebbels, and Höss, men like the courteous, well-dressed Nazi Franz Stangl who'd talked for more than seventy hours running to the journalist, Gitta Sereny, hardly blinking his eyes or licking his lips. For six straight days he'd talked, this son of a night-watchman, this Kommandant of Sobibor, this Nazi Franz Stangl, sometimes cracking his knuckles, sometimes arching his back, his lips moving, her pencil scratching, even when his shoulders had slumped, when the hour was late, even when his mouth had drooped, when Sereny herself had had to stifle her yawns, lighting one cigarette after another to keep herself attentive, alert, even then, when he'd been served his meals, he could order what he liked, he'd kept talking, hardly even shifting in his chair, hardly blinking his eyes, his back straight, his nails clean, his cuffs and collars white. Each day, in the fine soft German of his native Austria, he'd filled the little room with his brooding, his words, his teeth flashing, his lips smacking, his mouth and jaw moving, like a puppet's always moving, sometimes in the effort to chew his food, the beef and potatoes he preferred, but mostly in the effort to keep talking, after all food was just food. For more than seventy hours running he'd talked and talked to the

journalist, Gitta Sereny, or rather *at* her, *through* her, she
might have been pillar, a doorway, a block, the same sort
of block used to construct the modern block room in
which they'd sat talking that spring, in which, over a series
of days, while the rain poured down outside, the Nazi
Franz Stangl, had held forth for more than seventy hours
running to the historian, Gitta Sereny, who'd listened
calmly, where she'd sat facing him across the small pine
table, hardly breathing, hardly moving, for fear of distract-
ing him, of making him scruple, of making him *think*. Day
after day, as the clock had ticked, as the radiator had hissed
and gurgled beside them, she'd listened to him without
expression or reply, never groaning or sighing, never
smirking, never even sucking her teeth. In the seventy odd
hours she'd listened to him that April, she'd refused to take
her eyes off him, never shifting her position there, at the
little pine table, except to write, to make a note of something or to light a cigarette, she'd smoked so much her
throat had burned. In the seventy odd hours she'd listened
to him, this master-weaver, this mechanical engineer, this
Nazi Franz Stangl, she'd done her best to conceal herself,
her thoughts, her feelings, to dissolve herself *as herself*,
shedding all that was her, that had been, in her effort to
expunge herself completely, to see him plainly, without
hatred or bias—though she'd detested him, every bit of

him: his lips, his tongue, his craven, hackneyed phrases, *I was just following orders, I did nothing wrong, my conscience is clear.* She'd suffered each and every moment just to look at him, this Nazi Franz Stangl, this Kommandant of Treblinka, this murderer of 870,000 Jews, to consider his red-rimmed eyes, his fine grey sweater, his broad red hands with their neatly clipped nails. For more than seventy hours running she'd withstood his gloating and boasting, his taunts and provocations, *what about Dresden and Hiroshima, what about Vietnam.* For the sake of her work, for the sake of posterity, she'd vowed to thwart him at every turn, to resist his stratagems, his games, she'd not be baited by him but would efface herself completely, but cipher, a scribe, listening only to the sounds he made, he might have been a kettle or freight train or bird, listening keenly, if vacantly, the way a tape recorder listens, like the softly whirring tape recorder on the chair by her side, onto the dark magnetic tape of which each word, each phrase, of the Nazi Franz Stangl was leaving its marking, its print. With her cigarette in her cigarette holder she'd studied him closely, there in that modern block room, this husband, this father, this Nazi Franz Stangl. In the more than seventy hours she'd listened to him talking, that spring, she'd studied him more closely than she'd ever studied anyone before, his receding gray hair, his dark ties and white shirts. She'd studied his eyes and nose, his lips, his tongue, his teeth, and over time his voice—that voice!—had unmade her, a voice so smug, so remorseless, she'd wanted to spit in his face. My mother had told me all about Gitta Sereny and the Nazi Franz Stangl, about the way the Nazis had loved to talk—*and still do*, in their letters and diaries, in their telegrams and memoranda, in the books and films and articles about them, and in the literally thousands of pages of courtroom transcripts, they keep talking and talking, she'd despaired, when exhausted by her thinking, her work. Covering her ears, she'd pleaded, Will they ever be silent? Will they ever be still? It's a story I'd often told Teresa, she'd often asked me to tell it to her, the story of Gitta Sereny and the Nazi Franz Stangl, and of my mother crying and tearing at her hair. I remembered I'd told Hans the story, too, where we'd sat together in the little garden at the Delacroix Museum, the story of Gitta Sereny and the tape recorder and the Nazi Franz Stangl, and I remembered the particular look in his eyes, the retreat, the incomprehension, an expression, a momentary absence in his face, his being, that had told me at once he hadn't heard it before, nor obviously read that part in her book, the part about the journalist Gitta Sereny and the Nazi Franz Stangl who'd all but talked himself to death. For some reason my mother had never told Hans the story, had never mentioned the way, some nights, the Nazis had screeched and chattered like monkeys in her head. I was thinking about my mother, about the fact that she hadn't told him that story, and wondering what had restrained her, what impulse, what fear, when I was shaken from my musing by the sound of someone speaking German just behind me, a man, a Berliner, by the sound of him, saying something about a brand of toothpaste he liked. It was jarring, his voice—the 'icks", the soft g's—and it was everything I could do to resist the urge to turn around and glare at him. Instead, I tried to catch his reflection in the window but could make out little more than the blurry features of the woman seated beside him. Reflexively I covered my ears, for I couldn't bear the sound of it—the pitch, the accent, the language itself; it grated on my nerves. *Muttersprache und Mördersprache.* Even when my mother had spoken it on the telephone at night, to one of her friends or colleagues in Berlin, her voice dreamy, naïve, the door to her room left ajar so that the light had cut a long, bright line down the hallway, even then I'd cringed to hear it, had feared it, suspected something else, something curled moistly within the smooth dark shell of that tongue, so that it came as a relief to me when, abruptly, the man behind me stopped talking, no doubt to listen to some music or to watch a video on his laptop or phone.

Head back, I took a deep breath and sighed. I was surprised by my agitation. I read in German every day, often for hours at stretch, though it had been a while, I realized, since I'd heard it spoken at my ear. Somehow, for some reason, it had caught me off guard. Rattled, I peered out the window, hoping to determine where we were on the journey, how far we'd come from Paris, but couldn't recognize a thing. We passed a farm, a small, sullen-looking church, then a cluster of ancient gray-stone houses abandoned to the rain, when I was startled by what looked like a spray of surf at the window, as if the train was surging down the coast of France, along the surf line, the broad, gray fields the ocean itself, though it was only a spray of small, white-lit birds against the pale gray sky, a spray of pale, white-lit birds that had been startled by the train, not the surf at all, the ocean, but merely a flock of small, startled birds that had startled me from my thinking with their resemblance to ocean spray, to the great white plumes of spray cast up where the ocean strikes the rocks along the western coast of France to where my mother had liked to take me when I was young. In the months before Teresa's death, she'd often asked me to tell her about our trips there, to Brittany, to the Côte Sauvage with its cold and silvery light. Time and again, she'd asked me about our train ride from Paris to Vannes, about the things we saw and felt, about the bus to Quiberon. She'd liked to hear about the rocks and surf there, to picture my mother perched high upon the rocks in the wind and rain. At Teresa's bidding, I'd often told her about the rocks and surf at Quiberon, and about the quiet evenings there, with my mother, in the modest Hôtel de la Mer. She'd liked to hear about the small hotel in which we'd stayed, in which, after a dinner of fish and winkles in the restaurant downstairs, I'd followed my mother back to our room, where, if it was cold out, if the night was too windy for a walk along the beach, she'd drink her wine in a chair by the window and read aloud to me from whatever book she was reading at the time, mostly novels by women, glinting, splintered tales by Jaeggy, Rhys, and Taubes, by Quin, Duras, and Ernaux. I remembered one night in particular, a night about which I'd often told Teresa, a night of wind and rain when my mother had read aloud to me a section of the novel she was reading at the time, the title of which I've never managed to recall, though years later I'd asked her about it, and had even searched the books on her shelves for it, once she was dead. In the scene my mother had read aloud to me, a woman with a limp was in a gallery looking at a painting by Bonnard, a brightly colored painting of a dining room with a view of a garden and of the sea, when she was startled from her reverie by the sudden, wraith-like appearance of a girl in the canvas itself, a young woman at the right-hand side of the painting who—in her coloring, her essence—seemed both separate from and a part of the painted wall. Help! cried the girl in the painting to the woman in the gallery, the woman in the novel my mother was reading aloud to me. I've been trapped here by my crazy father! Please, you must help me, she begged. You must alert the authorities, let someone, *anyone*, know! The woman in the gallery was surprised to be so addressed by a figure in a painting and lurched back from the wall. She felt silly, embarrassed, and looked anxiously about her, for she'd never talked to a painting before. But why not just climb out the window? she whispered to the girl, at length, nearly pressing her lips to the paint. Because I can't! claimed the girl. Don't you see? The table, the window, the garden—it's all an illusion, a trick! Even later, when Teresa and I were together there, in Brittany, in Quiberon, where she'd persuaded me to take her one winter, when she was feeling restless and glum, even then, after we ourselves had stood on the rocks in the wind and spray, when later we were warm and dry and settled for the night in our room in the modest Hôtel de la Mer, even then she'd asked me to tell her the story about the girl in the painting, and about my mother herself, about the music she'd liked, about the clothes she'd

worn, about the thoughts—those inklings—that had rattled all day in her brain. Had she shaved her legs? Had she
worn perfume? Had she paid her bills on time? It seemed
there'd been nothing about my mother that hadn't interested her, that hadn't signaled something greater, something more. I remembered the way she'd handled my
mother's books, the few of them I'd kept on a shelf by my
desk, sniffing them, inspecting them, only to run her fingers along their weathered spines as if decoding some
secret, some message in braille. Among other things, I'd
saved my mother's favorite ashtray, the one she'd kept on
the corner of her desk, a chipped crystal ashtray from the
Sevilla-Biltmore in Havana where, she'd once told me,
she'd stayed when she was young. Teresa, for reasons I
could never grasp, had been obsessed with it, often pick-
ing it up from its place on the mantelpiece to examine its
faded red lettering and seal, only to hold it like a prism to
the light. Sadly, there was little I could tell her about the
ashtray, or about my mother's time in Cuba, who she was
with, what she was doing there, she might have been
twenty or ten. For some reason, I still don't understand it,
I'd told her mother about the ashtray, one night, not long
after Teresa's funeral. We'd been talking about my mother,
about her summers in Norway, when I'd told María
Pascuala about her daughter's obsession with my mother,

whom Teresa had never met, about her obsession with my mother's things, with her books and her lipsticks, and her chipped glass ashtray that I kept on shelf by my desk. Every day, for more than three weeks running, I'd sat there with María Pascuala at her bedside, in her darkly shuttered room, I'd talked with her about her daughter, I'd plumped her pillows, I'd listened to the voices—cold, implacable voices—on the old German radio she kept by her head. She'd spoken mostly in Spanish to me, a language I'd never really known, and with which I was helpless without Teresa, though for years I'd longed to speak it, to think like Teresa had thought, to live—but for an instant—within the lobes and folds of her queerly fashioned brain. My only reprieve, in my time there in Madrid, had been the hours when María Pascuala had rested, Andolça Mira standing guard at her door, a brief hiatus each day that had allowed me to escape into the streets, to walk and walk, only to find a bar filled with strangers, where the beer and company were cheap. Once out of her apartment, I'd tried not to think of anything or—the same thing—to think of everything at once, overtaxing my senses, my grief. Now I closed my eyes again, stretching my legs beneath the seat in front of me. I felt a warmth in my chest, then a tingling in my feet, my toes, when suddenly the woman beside me was shaking me awake. Here,

I thought you might be hungry, she said, setting before me a small cardboard tray. For each of us, she'd purchased a sandwich and a miniature bottle of wine. In fact I was hungry, I was very hungry, and thanked her profusely, tearing open the sandwich wrapper, then pouring myself some wine. You must have been pretty tired, she remarked with a smile. One minute I'm telling you about this painting I'd heard about—you're nodding your head, you're looking right at me—and the next thing I know you're fast asleep! Surely you read about it, it was in all the papers, a painting called 'Winter' or 'The Skaters' that was stolen by the Nazis in 1933 and only recently discovered in a small museum in upstate New York! Quite a story, I'd say. I mean, what are the odds? That's what I love about it, the odds. She took a bite of her sandwich and frowned. It's funny, I've never liked ham. I'm not sure why I chose it today, I could have had turkey or cheese, though I see you like it fine! And why not? It seems that everyone likes ham these days. The French like it, the Germans like it, the Italians like it. And the Spanish—why, they're positively mad about it! My daughter says there's no escaping it there, that everywhere they go there's someone shoving ham in their faces! Obviously, her fiancé won't touch it, he can't, so that now he dreads going out for fear that some-one will offer him some ham! Obligingly I smiled, then checked my watch. We'd been traveling for just over two hours, through about half of which I'd slept, so that now my mind was considerably clearer. I knew that at any moment the train would begin slowing down for the repairs being made to the tracks up ahead. While normally such a delay would have irritated me, it didn't bother me at all. Indeed I felt happy, at ease, the sun shining, the sky blue, the fields and hedgerows now a deep and vital green. I was thinking of Valence, the next stop on the route, of its cathedral of old Roman stones, of its famous Maison des Têtes, when sure enough the train began to slow down, until all at once we were there, at the station itself. Apparently the work had ended just before our arrival, a fact not lost on the passengers bound for there who now hurried to gather their things. I watched them as they made their way out onto the platform, pressing their way through the crowd of lightly dressed people milling about in the frank southern sunshine. Years ago, Teresa and I had remarked these people, at least people like them, when we'd stopped for lunch here on our way to Aigues-Mortes. From our table on the sunny Place des Clercs, we'd marveled at the easy, satisfied way they'd walked and talked, as though we'd never seen their kind before. I remembered Teresa had eaten heartily that day, cheese and salad and dessert, after which we'd explored the modest city center on foot, admiring the shops, the plashing fountains, the bright, sweeping views of the Rhône. And before we'd left Valence we'd bought one of its famous Pogne brioches, a large, crown-shaped bread lightly flavored with orange blossom and rum, which we'd nibbled from the bag for the remainder of the trip. We'd driven straight to Aigues-Mortes, so that Teresa could photograph the salt pans there, the vast salt flats that had been used to cultivate the mineral since the time of the ancient Romans. One of the magazines she'd worked for at the time, a glossy culinary magazine, had planned a feature article on the city and its salt, known round the world as fleur de sel. Once there, there'd been nothing much to see, though Teresa's editor had been pleased with her shots and had paid her handsomely for them. As we'd been in no hurry to return to Paris, we'd had made our way back to Nîmes, along a series of winding country roads, where, feeling flush, we'd splurged on a room at the Hotel Imperator, just a short walk from the ancient Arènes and the Maison Carrée. Teresa had been so charmed by the city, by its warmth and light, and by its distinctly Spanish character, that we'd actually spoken with a realtor about renting an apartment for the following summer. I remembered we'd talked a lot about the ancient Romans that day. Teresa had read a number of books about them, about their governance and law, their architecture and engineering, and about the life and culture of Gallia itself, as the province had been known. It was her idea to visit the Pont du Gard, near Remoulins, the most stately of the many bridges that once comprised the great aqueduct that had supplied the water for the many baths and fountains of Nîmes. I remembered the bridge, its massive yellow blocks, and the light, like drops of gold, on the shallow, placid river that day. And I remembered our waiter at lunch, a portly young man named Achille, who'd told us about a little-known sinkhole not far from there, into the depths of which we might climb, if we were feeling adventurous. Located on the flatland above a little town called Dions, the sinkhole was larger than we'd expected. Standing at its rim, all we we'd been able to see within it were the dark green crowns of trees. As instructed by our waiter, we'd followed the trail around to the far side, where we'd found the start of a nearly overgrown path that vanished into the darkness below. Teresa hadn't hesitated, climbing nimbly down the trail ahead of me by using the roots and branches to steady her way. While the terrain around the sinkhole was hot and arid, devoted mostly to growing cherries and grapes, the air within it was thick and humid, so that by the time we'd reached the cave at bottom our skin had glistened with sweat. The memory was stirring, so much so that I winced with sorrow, only to feel a tugging at my sleeve. It was the woman seated beside me. She had a quizzical look on her face. Are you married? she repeated, a little too loudly, as the man across the aisle looked up at us. Married? I said. I glanced at the ring on my finger. Yes, I am. I mean, no, I *was* married. My wife, Teresa, is dead. The woman seated beside me thought about it for a moment, then shook her head. You must have loved her very much, she said. The platitude surprised me, the presumption of it, so that for moment I merely gaped at her. For all she knew, I'd hated my wife and was happy she was dead. The truth was, I was tired of it all—the looks, the sighs, the empty consolation. Everywhere I turned it was the same: people drawn to my suffering like moths to a flame. I could feel my anger rising and was about to get up, to go to the bathroom before I said something cruel, when the woman beside me sniffled, dabbing her eyes with her napkin. Her hands, I noticed, were trembling. I was about to speak, to say something to console her, when she stammered, I'm sorry, really. It's none of my business. It just seemed you knew." Knew? Knew *what*? I felt like screaming. I had no idea what she was talking about and glared at her as she paused to polish the lens of her glasses. It was something Teresa might have said to me, indeed had said at some point, at some time, in some other, different words. She'd often done that to me, made some remark that had left me gaping, unsettled, for days. We'd see a movie, attend a concert, or see an exhibition of new paintings by some rising young artist she knew, when I'd be struck by the impression, as I listened to her chatting with others, and with me alone at some nearby café, that she was being deliberately cryptic in her remarks, as if to exclude me, to keep me out. And that was where my logic had always failed me, for had she actually wanted to exclude me from that part of her life, to keep that other world of hers private, she needn't have invited me at all. She might have left me at home with my papers and books. Still, as much as I'd enjoyed our outings together, the chance to glimpse her other, more candid self, I could never escape the suspicion that was toying with me, testing me—and that somehow, nearly always, I'd failed. I felt it now—the regret, the anger, the disappointment in myself. The woman beside me cleared her throat, clearly to get my attention, so that I turned slightly to acknowledge her, when softly she explained, It's just these feelings I get. I've had them all my life. She smiled weakly at me. You see, I sensed it the instant I sat down beside you this morning, that you've a weight on your shoulders, that some nights you just look at your hands on the table and weep. I shook my head (What drivel! What nonsense!)

and was about to deny it, to reassure her, anything to divert her, to change the subject, when she said, Karl, my husband, he never knew. He never even looked at his hands. I noticed that as she spoke she was looking at her own, spotted in places and bare but for a thin gold ring. With their long, tapered fingers, I thought they were beautiful, when suddenly, mysteriously, it struck me: She and her daughter were estranged! Yes, that was it! The reception, the wedding…her daughter had no idea she was coming, that she was here right now on this train. I could not have explained how I knew it, what signs had given her away, though I was certain it was true. I felt it in my bones. Surreptitiously now I looked at her, where she sat there beside me, at her small, thin-lobed ear with its simple gold stud, the feathering of her lipstick, the slight, anxious bobbing of her head. There was something dark and concentrated in her that made me say: Will your daughter be meeting you at the station? I said it casually, as if by the way. To my surprise she smiled widely. Yes, of course she'll be meeting me! She says she's so excited about my arrival she can barely sleep. What with the wedding and all, and with her wanting to be certain I'll comfortable there, that I'll have everything I need. For her new apartment is small, very small. She fears I won't like it, that I'll find it too noisy, that Hakim's mother, Faiza, will make a fuss of some sort. Apparently she's prone to such things. Taken aback by her reply, I screwed up my eyes and considered her afresh. Her face had brightened so significantly at the mention of her daughter that it occurred to me I was wrong, that I'd misread the situation, but then she looked at her hands again. She twisted the bangles on her wrists. My Ellie, you know, she's quick to get worked up about things, she began, as if reluctant to admit it. She can make herself a nervous wreck. I told her I'd be happy to get a taxi at the station, that I'd be just fine in a hotel, for I know how busy she is, but she wouldn't hear of it, any of it. Apparently Hakim just bought a new car! she cried shrilly, anxiously, so clearly hurt by the fact of it, by its suggestion of a life apart from her own, that I squeezed her arm. Flushed with pity, I said, You know, it's true what you said about me, about my wife. I loved her very much. Some days I can barely breathe. And nothing ever changes. Every day it rains, every day I think, today will be different, but it never is, every hour, every minute, the same. I could feel the woman looking at me; I knew she was nodding her head. And I knew what was coming next. Where did we meet? I repeated. Right here on this train. On this route, anyhow. You see, I was returning from a conference in Barcelona, when she sat down beside me," I explained. The recollection was blinding and for an instant I closed my eyes. I said, All I really remember is that I felt hot and dizzy, as if the earth had just tipped and I was about to slide off! At that the woman beside me chuckled, clearly delighted, and it was my intention to end the conversation there, for I had said too much, actually popping in my ear pods to signal the fact to her, when to my surprise I added, She was killed in an accident. Crushed to death by a truck hauling bricks. How awful! gasped the woman beside me. Yes, she'd just had her hair done, I added absurdly, only to confess: No. No, I'm sorry. That's a lie It wasn't an accident at all. She killed herself one night. Jumped from the roof of her mother's building. She was only thirty-four. For a moment the woman beside me was silent. I thought I'd shocked her. I heard her sigh, heard the bangles at her wrists. Abashed, embarrassed, I waited a few beats, then stole a glance at her, expecting her to be staring at me, imploring me for more, but she was still engrossed with the messages on her phone. I felt the blood rush to my face. Fool! What was the hell the matter with me? I fumed inwardly. Why in the world had I told *her,* of all people, when I hadn't told anyone else? Not my sister, not my friends. What was I afraid of? A cold sweat had broken out on my back and suddenly my head began to throb, my vision faltered, my mouth and tongue went dry. At once I felt the train shudder, heard the screech of wheels, felt a pressure on my heart, my spine, when—for a dark and wrenching instant—I braced myself for the crash. Since Teresa's death, I'd frequently suffered such hallucinations, flashes of vertigo and nausea that often left me shaken for days. Fortunately the woman beside me hadn't noticed, still engrossed in her phone. I was ager to recover myself, and opened the novel *Malina* in my lap at random, hoping to focus my feelings, my thoughts, but was baffled by the German on the page:

> Reconciliation comes and drowsiness, my
> impatience softens, I wasn't secure but am
> once again safe, no longer walking past the
> Stadtpark at night, jittery as I walk along the
> facades of the buildings, no longer on a detour
> through the dark, but already a little at home,
> already docked safely at Ungargasse, already
> safe and sound in Ungargassenland, my head's
> already a little above the water even. Already
> gurgling the first words and sentences, already
> commencing, beginning...

I'd grabbed the book without thinking this morning, perhaps hoping it would be a comfort to me, a balm for my nerves, though I couldn't make sense of the words. I tried again, in another random place:

Yes, I read a lot, but the shocks, the things that
really stay with you are merely the vision of
a page, a remembrance of five words on the
lower left of page 27; Nous allons à l'Esprit.
Words on a poster, names on doors, titles of
books left in a store window, never sold, a
magazine ad discovered in the dentist's waiting room, a gravestone epitaph that struck my
eye: HERE LIES…

Bewildered, I closed the book; I turned it round in my hands. Years ago, Teresa had given it to me as a gift, a signed first edition of the novel. It was a handsome book, with its ivory-colored dust jacket, modern red font, and black and white photograph of the author herself, taken shortly before her death in Rome. I studied her face, the dark eyes, the wry smile, the graceful sweep of her straw-colored hair, and tried with all my might to recall the basic tale—the pain and longing, the stories trapped in stories, the dark roaring chaos of words. There was music, a princess, a bit of blue thread; there were phone calls and telegrams, Rorschach tests and Turk's-cap lilies, and—yes, of all things—a Jewish Serbian coat! I remembered that, and the fact that the narrator herself was writing a book, a fairy tale of sorts, in fact, the very book in my hands. Teresa had loved the novel, at least the Spanish version of it. After dinner she'd liked to read it at the kitchen table, with its faded blue oilcloth, nodding and sighing and sipping her Côtes du Rhône. I could picture her there, in her sweatpants and ratty green sweater, reading the novel, or some other such book, or else examining the photographs she'd taken that week, that day, most of which she'd shot for magazines, for which she'd be poorly, reluctantly paid, and some of which she'd taken for herself, with her 'other eye', photographs—she'd called them *auras*—of each of which (before she'd deleted it) she'd made but a single blurry print. I'd long felt that, for all her familiar qualities, she was fundamentally different from me, and from the people I knew, that she spent her days on some other, alternative plane, thinking and feeling things I could never hope to think, to witness, to feel. Even when she was looking right at me, talking to me, when we were eating and drinking together at the little table in her kitchen, there was something alien about her, something supernal, unearthly, aloof. The night I met her she'd seemed haunted to me, like a stranger from some other time and place. Only later, much later, had I discovered what now I am certain was at least a part of the reason why. Bored one night, as I'd waited for her to return from work, I'd taken up a paperback from the little bookcase by her side of the bed, a French edition of the collected letters of Rosa

Luxemburg, and was flipping idly through the pages, on some of which certain lines had been marked in pencil or pen, when I'd noticed the book had been inscribed. The message—apparently some lines from a poem—was so intimate, so explicit, I'd gasped: "Night opens itself only once. It's enough. You see. You've seen." Below it the author had drawn an eye, then signed her name beneath it. Sick at heart, I'd read the inscription again; I'd studied the tiny eye. Mila? Who was this 'Mila'? I'd fretted, searching the book for more clues. Teresa had never mentioned her before, I would have remembered it, and wracked my brain that night, as I lay beside her in bed, trying to recall her various friends and acquaintances from over the years, some of whom I'd known, and some of whom I'd only met in passing and had never seen again, yet would have remembered by name. For weeks it had troubled me, the identity of this woman, this blind spot in my knowledge of Teresa. Not that I'd ever really known her in the first place. When it came to her past, to the places she'd lived, to the people she'd known, she'd always been guarded with me, in fact so vague, so circumspect in her stories about herself that I'd never felt certain, at ease. Weeks had passed, life had distracted me with other matters, when one day, while searching for a pen in her desk, I'd happened upon a photograph, a snapshot of a slender young woman with shaggy, blonde hair sitting on a rock somewhere in the sun. Even in the photograph the woman had seemed to radiate a kind of energy and light. It was Mila—I'd known it at once, had felt it like a wound in my chest. All that day I'd studied the photograph, holding it up to the light, turning it this way and that, only to prop it against the books on my desk, as if the woman might confide in me, as if, with patience, with faith, she might speak. I'd thought briefly of destroying the photograph (Teresa would never have suspected me), but had been thwarted by the look in Mila's eyes. When finally I'd screwed up the courage to ask Teresa about it, I'd found her standing at the window in our bedroom in only a t-shirt and underwear. It was summer, nighttime, the window was open, the room airless and hot. "Mila?" she'd repeated, taking a long, deep drag of her cigarette. I couldn't tell what she was looking at, what she was thinking. By the angle of her head I'd supposed she was staring at the construction site on the sidewalk below, where for weeks municipal crews been working to replace a large black pipe. She'd been especially moody of late; I'd come home, on numerous occasions, to find her watching television, a pastime that had never interested her before. It hadn't seemed to matter to her what sort of program was on (a game show, a soccer match, the evening news), her expression, her fixation, was the same. It was a habit that had lasted for days, she'd hardly spoken to me, subsisting mostly on crackers, raw carrots, and wine, when one evening I'd returned from the library to find she'd gone. She'd done it before—simply vanished, disappeared. As usual, she'd taken her laptop and a small leather duffel in which she'd stowed her cameras and clothes. I was always surprised by what she'd left behind, the books and journals, her door key, her earrings, her favorite pair of shoes. Each time she'd vanished I'd assumed she was off on assignment somewhere; I'd told everyone that. It had seemed plausible; it was the most I could fathom, could bear. Once returned, it was only seldomly, and usually in passing, that she'd ever told me where she'd been. We'd be admiring some pastries in the window of a shop, when she'd let slip that her childhood friend, Nicole, with whom she'd recently stayed in Calais, had taught her how to make them. Or—and this was more common—she'd suddenly break off in the middle of telling me a story to show me, on her camera, a photograph she'd taken of some market or alley or church. I'd never recognized the places, or rarely. It hadn't seemed to matter, they might have been photos of Mars. I recalled looking at her that night, where she'd stood smoking at the window in her underwear and t-shirt, and thinking I should curse her, smash her cameras—anything to shake her from the spell of herself. I'd wanted her to look at me, to beg my forgiveness, to weep like a child in my arms. Instead she'd flashed me a bitter smile. Mila? she'd repeated, as if tasting the word. No one, really. Just the love of my life! I remembered that I'd laughed. I'd assumed she was joking, that now she'd kiss me, reassure me, but she hadn't. Instead she'd pushed past me without a word, climbed into bed, then turned her face to the wall. Less than three weeks later she was dead. As subtly as possible now, I withdrew the photograph of Mila from the pocket where I kept it in my laptop case. Hardly a day had passed since Teresa's death when I hadn't looked at it, so that now her features were deeply familiar to me. In recent weeks she'd taken shape in my mind as someone still out there, still breathing, still acting upon the world in which I lived. Even when Teresa was alive, I'd often fantasized about meeting Mila, about encountering her by chance one day in a crowded shop or while waiting for the métro or bus. I'd have recognized her at once, I was sure. Yet it was more often at a café that my dreaming placed us. I'd be walking down the street, enjoying the afternoon, when I'd spot her sitting alone with a cup of coffee, engrossed in a newspaper or book. She'd dressed variously on those occasions, sometimes in jeans and sandals, sometimes in a skirt and t-shirt, sometimes in espadrilles and an Indian-patterned dress. The instant I approached her she'd look up; I'd smile, introduce myself, and soon we'd be talking and laughing as friends. We'd sit for hours that way, sometimes chatting, sometimes reading, sometimes just gazing mutely at the traffic on the avenue. Of course I'd liked her at once; I'd suspected I would. I'd liked her naked face, her limpid eyes, her boyish, unkempt hair. She was from Vlorë, from Kraków, from Split, it changed each time we met, though her accent was usually the same. In my dreams of her there were certain English words and expressions I liked to hear her say, so that some days I'd quizzed her about art or the weather or the state of public transportation with no other purpose than to get her to repeat them. She'd seemed to enjoy the game, sometimes resisting the particular idiom or word I was after until I myself was forced to say it, when with her lighter she would tap the table and laugh. On some occasions, I'd bring her back to my apartment, she was curious to see it, to know how Teresa had lived. I'd show her the locks on the door, which Teresa had hated; she'd liked the idea of neighbors—even strangers—walk-ing in. There in the little kitchen, I'd open the curtains for Mila, I'd make her some tea. I'd never minded when she'd explored the place on her own, appraising the spices in the rack by the stove, my appointments on the calendar, and the empty bird cage in the bedroom window, designed to look like a cottage, with its gable-style roofs. She'd noticed little things, *everything*, the chips in the tiles, the creaks in the floorboards, the cracks in the ceilings and walls. I'd watched her as she'd traced the moldings, touched the doorknobs and light switches. And I'd delighted in the fairytale way she'd tested the furniture—the loveseat, the coffee table, the old ladderback chair in the hall. In some of my dreams of Mila, we'd spent whole days together sorting Teresa's things—her books and photographs, her necklaces and rings, her blouses, skirts, and shoes. And some nights, if it was late, if it was raining outside, we'd lie together in bed, listening to music, both hers and mine, to Bach and Clara Schumann, to Miles Davis and Clifford Brown, musing mutely, chastely, about strange and negligible things. And some nights, when the space around us had seemed to swell with the weary conscience of the world, I'd tell her about the poets Bachmann and Celan, and about Teresa's obsession with them, with their letters, their love, sharing with Mila one of their missives in particular, I had to, it had haunted Teresa, a curt if gnomic message from Celan to his 'Inge' marked *Lavallois, 7 July 1951*:

> In the place where we thought we stood,
> thoughts work in the name of the heart—but
> not vice versa. The fact that precisely the

opposite happened cannot undo a gesture,
even if it was the only one still possible in a
difficult moment. Nothing is repeatable; our
time, our lifetime, halts only once, and it is
terrible to know when and for how long.

There in my apartment, I'd describe for her the way Teresa had puzzled over the passage for hours at a stretch. It had troubled her—she'd wracked her brain over it—to imagine what Bachmann, poor woman, had felt. And soon we'd be reveling in Teresa's quirks and eccentricities: the way she'd slept erratically, had hoarded her things, and had often gone for days without eating, only to spend hours in her tiny kitchen, baking breads, roasting meats, chopping fruits and vegetables, and shucking oysters by the dozens, which she'd arranged for herself, as in a restaurant for children, on brightly colored plates. She'd liked to sing to herself—Mila might remember that, some nights, only to grow quiet and close her eyes. Often, when I'd bring her back to the apartment with me, she'd liked just to listen to me talk about Teresa, her eyes closed, her legs folded neatly beneath her. Eager to be candid with her, to win her confidence, her trust, I'd recount everything I could remember about Teresa, about her mother, her childhood, about the way she'd spent whole days reading feverishly in her large stuffed chair by the window or on the dusty floor of one of the many old bookshops in town. There was one shop in particular where I'd usually been able to find her sitting or squatting at the end of the same darkly cluttered aisle. Surrounded by novels, and by tattered volumes of poetry, philosophy, and art, it often took her minutes to notice me, my sense my presence there beside her. I'd made a point of not disturbing her, if I could help it, sometimes reading, sometimes just pretending to read, so that I could watch her at my leisure, trace the shadows on her wan, inscrutable face. She'd never seemed unhappy at my appearance, I'd explain to Mila, though there were occasions when she hadn't seemed to see me at all, abruptly gathering up the books she'd chosen and pushing her way past me, as if in the moment, in the grip of her reading, only the books in her hands were substantial, were real. She'd had a way of concentrating, of withdrawing into herself, that had made me think of certain mystics and nuns. When so disposed, she could go for hours without so much as glancing at me, editing her photographs, reading her books, and chatting easily with her friends and compatriots on the phone. Some days I'd simply watched her, as though she were a character in a film, standing beside her as she brushed her teeth and used the toilet, as she showered and got dressed, only to trail her down the stairs to the street. On such days she'd walked slowly, stopping here and there to greet someone she knew or to peer into a restaurant or shop, only to press her way, with a sudden resolution, through the midday throngs of people, so that I'd had to run to keep up with her. She'd never chased me away, I'd have obliged her at once, torn always between my desire to punish her for her indifference to me and by the chance to study her frankly, with impunity, recording in the tiny notebook in my brain all of the little things that had distinguished her, that had made her so winsome, so strange. She'd had a way of squinting her eyes and holding her breath, not in the effort to see more clearly, but as if to prepare herself for something unpleasant, such as the removal of a bandage or the prick of a doctor's needle. She'd not been aware of it, it had happened too often for that, so that each time she'd screwed up her eyes that way I'd surveyed the vicinity around her, hoping to detect what had triggered it, the reaction, what object or person, what sunbeam, what flavor, what sound. Yet to no avail. As with most of her impulses, the source of the tic had seemed internal, an essential part of her wiring, her brain. She'd had other habits, too, of which she may or may not have been conscious. She'd sucked her teeth, she'd twisted her hair, and she'd fondled her earlobes whenever I'd read aloud to her at night. Each time I'd read aloud to her, it had been only a matter of minutes before she'd begun to stroke one or the other of her earlobes, I'd noticed it at once, the way she'd kneaded the soft white flesh between her fingers like a fetish or talisman, like a tiny ball of dough. And soon I'd felt her body relax beside me, heard her breathing soften, as if, with the simple gesture of stroking her earlobes, she'd induced in herself a kind of stupor or trance. Then again, it hadn't been like that at all, I'd explain to Mila, for always Teresa had been keenly aware of me. If I'd omitted a line or detail in my reading of some letter or telegram she'd heard before, if my translation of it had seemed careless, impatient, if I'd neglected to define some allusion, a reference to some person, time, or place, if for an instant the feeling had faltered in my voice, as it had when I'd been tired or distracted, she'd challenged me at once, appraising me sharply with her large green eyes. Then, too, there'd been nights when we'd merely talked about the writers themselves, about Bachmann and Celan, nights when she hadn't wanted me to read aloud to her, but only to tell her about the poets, about their writing, their suffering, their love. Yet it was for Bachmann alone that she'd reserved her greatest faith—Bachmann the fey, the feral, the fractious poet-martyr burned alive in her bed:

> When I, crowned with smoke,
> know again, whatever happens,
> my bird, my nightly accomplice,

when I am ablaze at night,
a dark grove begins to crackle
and I strike the sparks from my body.

There in Rome, Teresa had quoted the lines to me, like a mantra, a charm. She'd known exactly where the poet had died, leading me by the hand, along the cobbled Via Giulia, to Palazzo Sacchetti, before which we'd stood that bright winter day to admire the weathered facade with its coat of arms and finely chiseled inscription: TV MIHI QVODCVMQVE HOC RERVM EST. Built in 1542 by Antonio da Sangallo the Younger, the once-sumptuous palace had been converted into apartments by the time Bachmann had settled there. Cold, collars up, we'd circled the building once, then twice, wondering which of all the windows had been hers. And later, by the nearby Tiber, beneath a sky of Roman swallows, we'd talked of life and death. Teresa had told me many things that day—that marble could breathe (she'd had me press my ear to a pillar), that Proust had hated pasta, that she knew she dissolved me, some days, like sugar on her tongue. And she'd told me about the dream she'd had one night, a dream in which my mother was the writer Ingeborg Bachmann. It was silly, she'd insisted, she'd been quick to make light of it, hooking her arm through mine and leading me south along the river to find a warm caffè. It was a dream she'd had before, she'd confessed, a dream in which my mother was the writer Ingeborg Bachmann, in which the three of us had lived happily ever after, there in Paris, just a block from Paul Celan. There by the Tiber, Teresa had told me all about her dream of my mother with the look of someone still dreaming it, describing for me, in ways I'd found troubling, uncanny, my mother's loneliness and depression, her smoking and pacing, the way she'd grieved like a child at the sound of evening rain. And she'd told me of how my mother had suffered on the days when she couldn't see Celan, the way she'd ground her teeth and pulled at her hair whenever he was busy with his work, his wife, pacing the drafty rooms of our apartment, unable to think, gulping fish-like at the dark and fetid air, as she'd awaited a signal from him, a code, a message, any sign that he'd thought of her at all—a ticket stub, a coin or button he'd found in the gutter one day, even a word he'd liked and had scribbled on a napkin or matchbook for her, or on the back of one of his morbid, 'word-poor' poems, a draft of which he'd completed in the black milk of daybreak that morning and had tucked into her mailbox, or had paid someone to deliver to her, to climb the narrow stairs to our apartment and hand to her in the guise of something useful, something else. Hunched over caffè corretti back in our hotel in Rome, Teresa had described for me the very apartment in which we'd lived: the sofa by the door, the dictionary in the bathroom, even my mother's bedroom-cum-study with its green-speckled curtains, mustard-colored chair, and cheaply framed reproduction of Dumonstier's 'Right Hand of Artemisia Gentileschi' on the wall by her desk. And the views. Teresa had sketched for me the very views from our windows there (the corner, the cornice, the church), had described for me in detail the broken old chair by the door, even the layout of our kitchen, our dreary little kitchen, a room she'd never seen before but *knew*: the pale stenciled cabinets, the round Formica table, the small gas range with its simple burners and bright red knobs, the very range with which my mother had gassed herself to death one night, while I was out drinking with friends, when, having found herself alone, after a long day of writing, of thinking, she'd shut up the room, opened the valves, and laid her head on the table to sleep. For some reason, she'd taken down the phone book, perhaps to place a call, but to whom, to say what? I didn't know, I couldn't even guess, and winced at the pain in my chest. Breathless, anxious now, I searched blindly out the window for something, anything, on which to focus my eyes, some object or thing that would bind me to the present, the earth. My pulse was racing, I could feel it, my mouth was dry, and I thought I might be sick, so that I was relieved to hear the familiar chiming of the little speaker above my head, followed at once by the prerecorded voice announcing that Nîmes would be the next stop on the line. Nîmes! The name itself seemed a sign to me, a cry. Why not just get off there? I considered rashly, when the idea bloomed fully in my mind. What was to stop me? I glanced at the woman beside me. I wasn't scheduled to teach again until the fall, I might even extend my leave, no one would miss me, no one would care. I could live anywhere I liked, work anywhere I pleased. I remembered one of the apartments Teresa and I had seen when we were there, in Nîmes, a gloomy old place near the university with a dark galley kitchen and large stained sink. I'd live simply, invisibly, reading and writing, and eating bread and olives on the terrace in the sun. Without the rain and distractions of Paris, I could finish this book of mine, get a draft to my editor sometime later this fall. Anxiously I checked my watch. We were due to arrive in exactly twelve minutes. Twelve minutes. I peered out the window, I felt for my wallet and phone. I considered my bag on the rack above my head. It'd be simple: all I'd have to do was to gather my things and get off. Turning slightly toward the woman beside me, I considered what I'd say: *Excuse me, but I've decided to stop here in Nîmes. It's just occurred to me. I mean, what the hell, right? You only live once!* Unhappy with the lines, I repeated them in my head, in different voices, different tones, even shrugging my shoulders for emphasis, yet the result was the same. I needed to keep it simpler, be myself: *Excuse me, but I've decided to stop here in Nîmes. I've got a couple days before I'm due in Madrid and I'd like to look around a bit. See the old amphitheater, the Maison Carrée. I'm told there's a temple in the gardens that's nice.* Yes, surely that was better, more like me, I reflected. I was hardly the reckless type. Again I checked the time, peered out the window, and was relieved to see that the train's speed had not yet decreased. In the distance, beyond a stand of Italian cypresses, I could make out a tract of modern-style homes, the sort found everywhere in the States. We passed a series of vineyards and fields, an old farmhouse, a man on a new blue tractor, when suddenly the train began to slow down. Some housing blocks appeared, a large metal shed, then a long line of freight cars in a siding, when again I heard the chiming from the speaker above my head. We'd arrived at the station in Nîmes. It was now or never, I thought. I heard the passengers shifting around me, murmuring, collecting their things. The retired plumber across the aisle was tightening the laces of his boots. In another minute the doors of the train would be opened and he would get off.

No doubt his wife was here waiting for him. I tried to picture her, her kerchief, her cheeks, but was distracted by the feeling in my stomach, my head. I stared madly at my phone. Did I actually have the courage to do it, to excuse myself and get off? I didn't think so, I feared not, though in the instant I couldn't help imagining it—the thrill of stepping out onto the platform, the warmth and sunlight on my skin. I'd take a taxi to the city center, sit for a coffee and a glass of wine in the Place de l'Horloge, then make my way through the parched yellow streets to some nearby hotel for the night. My palms were sweaty, I could feel my heart beating. What was I afraid of? I berated myself. Was there really anything at stake? All I had to do was get off. I could always catch another train tomorrow, I reasoned simply, yet still I didn't move, my feet all but rooted to the floor. I knew that Teresa wouldn't have hesitated, she'd have gathered our things and dragged me off the train. Why was I so timid, so weak? I heard the doors open with a hiss, watched the passengers as they pressed their way down the aisle. I knew it was hopeless, that I would never get off. I simply didn't dare. Bitter, disgusted with myself, I twisted the flesh on my arm, hoping that the pain would compel me to my feet, but I didn't rise, I hardly felt a thing. Instead I watched as the last of the passengers filed out onto the sunny platform, when again I heard the chiming from the speaker and the doors hissed closed. Blindly I stared at the novel in my hand. My breathing was easier now and I closed my eyes. With a lurch the train began to move again. I knew I'd been kidding myself. Not for an instant had I actually *intended* to get off the train. I'd lived too long with myself to think I could ever be so swayed. Still I couldn't deny the excitement I'd felt, the twinge of danger, the lure of the unexpected, so that it was with a fractured relief that I studied the ancient, sun-bleached city as we snaked our way through it—the narrow streets, the scattered palm trees, the billboards and graffiti, the proud, if neglected old mansions that still lined the tracks. My decision, I knew, had had nothing to do with fear, with daring, but had been a matter of plain common sense. After all, I'd promised my mother-in-law she'd see me this evening. I pictured her there in her bed, listening to one of her Catholic radio programs. She liked it when I plumped her pillows for her, when she could practice her English on me, harrying me with questions about America, about our guns and supermarkets, about Mexicans, Blacks, and Jews. In any case, what would I have done with myself in Nîmes? My money was limited; I didn't know a soul. Surely I'd have been lonelier than ever. We passed a long flowering hedge, then a soccer field on which some children were flying a kite. As with most cities, the outskirts were fairly nondescript; I might have been anywhere in the world for the apartment blocks, shopping centers, and warehouses, for the stark, random wastelands made by train tracks, highways, and drains. The woman beside me was sleeping, I hadn't noticed it, her chest rising and falling, her nostrils flaring gently. I thought about her daughter, Ellie, in Barcelona, tried to imagine her expression when, to her mother, she opened the door. Shifting slightly now, I considered her, the graceful slope of her nose, the wrinkles around her eyes and lips. My friend Antoine had once insisted, where we'd sat drinking by the Seine one night, that what ultimately distinguished one human mouth from another had less to do with biology or genetics, or with the dubious constructs of ethnicity and race, than with the particular language one spoke. Chinese mouths were Chinese mouths, Spanish mouths Spanish mouths, and Russian mouths (I'd pictured Stalin's, Turgenev's) always and only Russian mouths. Again I considered her, the shape and color of her lips. So far we'd spoken mostly in English, though I could tell her French was good, very good, if spoken with an accent I couldn't quite place. I guessed she lived somewhere on the outskirts of Paris, somewhere like Massy, Nanterre, or Montreuil. Her mouth itself told me nothing. The train had picked up speed again. For years, while Teresa and I were together, I'd felt that I was an intimate part of things—of books and trains and history, of art and cell phones and sex, that the world itself had sprung from us, was *for* us, *about* us. Eager for distraction, I looked out the window at the hills and scattered houses, at the battered stands of cypresses, and was struck again by the sense that much had changed since then, that now the world lay elsewhere, busy with other people and things. At a loss as to how to pass the time remaining, I decided to do a little work, to rough out at least the next few letters between Bachmann and Celan. In the past year, I'd assembled all of their correspondence on my laptop, organizing it by date and place, including all of the glosses and annotations from the original German edition, an edition that had never been completed. The editor, a Berliner and poet, had choked to death one evening in a restaurant in Ghent. I'd met him once, at a conference in Frankfurt, after which he'd treated me to a glass of Apfelwein in one of the many taverns there. In the ensuing months we'd corresponded regularly, dull, mostly scholarly stuff, which nevertheless had proven useful to me in my work. The man, named Oskar, had never been married, but had lived alone with his cat above a late-night kebab house in Kreuzberg. Once or twice a month he'd had dinner with his dentist, an avid reader with whom he'd sometimes shared his work. On my laptop, I'm pleased to see that the next two letters in the series are brief. The first, from Bachmann to Celan, dated December 2, read simply:

> When are you coming, dear Paul? Send me a
> telegram from Tübingen so that I can pick you
> up. Only a few more days now…
>
> Ingeborg

The second, written by Celan to Bachmann three days later, is equally plain:

> The day after tomorrow, <u>Saturday</u>, I will be in
> Munich—visiting you, Ingeborg.
>   Could you come to the station? My train
> will arrive in Munich at <u>12:07</u>. If you cannot
> come, I will be pacing up and down outside
> your house in the Franz-Josefstr. half an
> hour later.
>   Tomorrow I shall be in Tübingen (address:
> Hotel Lamm or Osiander Bookshop).
>
> Two more days, Ingeborg.
>
>   Paul

It is the following letter that intrigues me, one—a longer one—I remembered reading to Teresa in bed:

Ingeborg, my dear Ingeborg—

I cast another look out of the train, you
had looked around too, but I was too far away.

Then it came and choked me, so wildly.

And then, when I went back to the compartment, some- thing very strange happened.
It was so strange that I entrusted myself to it,
for a very long stretch of the journey—I shall
describe it to you here as it came to me—but
you must already forgive me for acting in so
uncontrolled a fashion.

So, I was back in my compartment and
took your poems out of my briefcase. I felt I
was drowning in something completely transparent and bright.

When I looked up, I saw the young woman
who had the window seat take out a copy
of *Akzente*, the last issue, and start leafing
through it. She leafed and leafed, and my eyes
could fol low her leafing, because they knew
that your poems and your name would come.
Then they came, and the hand that had been
leafing paused. And I saw that there was no
more leafing, that her eyes were reading, again
and again. Again and again. I was so grateful.
Then I thought for a moment that it could be
someone who had heard you read, who had
seen you and recognized you.

And then I wanted to know. And asked.

And said that it had been you, before. And
invited the lady, a young writer who had sent a
manuscript to *Desch* in Munich, who also, she
told me, wrote poems, to have a coffee with me.
Then I heard how much she admired you.

I hardly said anything careless, Ingeborg,
but I think she had already guessed; it was an
experience for her.

Then I gave her my two volumes of poetry
and asked her to read them only after I had
left the train.

She was a young woman, maybe thir-
ty-five; I supposed she knows now, but I do
not think she will tell people. I really do not
think so. Do not be angry with me, Ingeborg.
Please do not be angry.

It was so strange, it was so completely out
of our world—the person to whom I owe the
experience will have known who was sitting
in front of her. Say something about it, one
word—please!

Now I also think you could send this
woman your greetings, here is her address:

Margot Hindorf
Cologne-Lindenthal
Dürener Str. 62

Send me a line in Paris, I will be there on
Wednesday.

In Frankfurt, it was eight o'clock, I
immediately called Frau Kaschnitz—no
one answered. I shall try it again tomorrow
morning.

I have to see you again, Ingeborg, for I
love you.

Paul

I am staying with Christoph Schwerin here:
our books are standing side by side.

There'd been something about the letter that had
puzzled Teresa. What it was she'd never managed to
say. Equally disconcerting to her had been Bachmann's
prompt, if peculiar reply:

Paul, dear,

here in the hotel I only have this crum-
pled-up paper, everything else is in the Franz
Josephstrasse with the candlestick. This afternoon I picked up your letter there. The story
is a strange and beautiful one; now it belongs
to us. Why should I be angry? But I will not
write to the woman, forgive me—I cannot add
anything of worth. (And I find it difficult to
write to others.)

In the evening, Monday evening, I went to
Piper with the black penny in my hand, and

everything went well; I was also able to move
to a hotel at once—I will be staying here (it is
called Blaues Haus) until Friday morning.

The telephone number was changed today.
The number, which will stay the same, is:
337519. You can cross out the other one.

Every day is now full of echoes. But you
must not neglect Gisèle because of me. Not
out of duty, but out of liberation.

Whom will we have to thank for
everything?

Ingeborg

Bachmann had been one of a few contemporary German-language writers whose work my mother had read with an almost holy devotion. In fact, I'd first encountered her name on the spine of one of my mother's books, the titles of which I used to peruse from where I sat on her bed beneath the large, drafty window. She hadn't minded if I sat there while she worked, though I'd been forbidden to talk to her if she was reading or typing or talking on the phone. If, on the other hand, she was only smoking or had turned to the window to check the weather or the time of day, I was free to say what I pleased. I often asked her about her books, about the ones on her desk, which she was currently consulting, and about the ones on her shelves, sometimes because I liked a particular title, its color, its font, sometimes merely to hear her talk about it, to watch her expressions as she flipped idly through the pages. For years I'd puzzled over one title in particular, that of Bachmann's fictional letters, *Briefe an Felician* or *Letters to Felician.* At the time, I'd thought 'briefe' meant brief, that perhaps Felician was a boy who'd died young, before his time, a boy of my nature, my age. Even after my mother had translated the title for me, I'd been unable to shake the idea that the character in the story was in danger, that if I opened the book he'd be dead. Out the window now came a flash of suburbs, of tract-style homes with swimming pools and brightly tiled roofs, followed shortly by a smattering of older villages with their blockish churches, ragged olive trees, and ugly, patchwork vineyards, and by the arid scrublands known as garrigues, with their fragrant tangle of juniper and oak, chicory and sage, rosemary, rockrose, and thyme. While in Nîmes, Teresa and I had spent a morning in the recently completed Musée de la Romanité, admiring its collection of steles, statues, bronze jars, oil lamps, arrowheads, javelin points, flint daggers, human skulls and jawbones, amulets, beads, and coins. In the giftshop there I'd purchased a book that had held me captive for days, Gustaf Sobin's *Luminous Debris,* a patient, often lyrical meditation on the history and landscapes of Provence and Languedoc. Even now I could recall certain words and phrases from it, a strange, unwonted vernacular that seemed to me as poetic, sacred, as it was practical, technical, profane, phrases, terms, like 'auroral moment', 'vestigial marker', 'terrain vague', and—my favorite, having to do with the wave patterns in certain Ionico-Massalian pottery, the stirring—'undulant-oblique'. At lunch in the café near the Pont du Gard the next day, I'd read aloud to Teresa the final chapter of Sobin's book, a coda of sorts, dedicated to the poet and member of the French Resistance, René Char, called 'Aquaeductus' in which the author compared the great conduit, now mostly ruined, to a fragmented antique text. Beginning at the springs near Uzès, at La Fontaine d'Eure, a source deemed salubrious by the ancient Romans, the aqueduct had carried the water, by means of a subtle gradient, and through miles of limestone piping, to the Pont du Gard, which straddled the Gardon River where we'd sat. According to Vitruvius, explained the author, the quality of the water source was best determined by the health and complexion of the local inhabitants, and by the simple test of sprinkling a few drops of it on a fine copper plate. If the drops left no stain then the water, claimed Vitruvius, was pure. It was through that very landscape that I was traveling now, my mind at ease with the warm, ragged colors, the light. I thought again of the author-expatriate Sobin, pictured him wandering the orchards and fields near his home in the hilltop village of Goult, to where he'd retreated to write his poetry, to think. I imagined him stopping here and there to kick at a clod of dirt or to squat down to examine some clue, some memento, he'd found, a bit of flint or ceramic or bone, some bright, vestigial marker of the region's secret, yet-incongruous past. On our last night in Nîmes, Teresa and I had been drinking wine at a bistro near the ancient amphitheater, when I'd persuaded her— the idea had just struck me—to let me take there, to Goult, on our drive back to Paris, though by then she was eager to return home and Sobin himself was long since dead. It had turned out to be a lovely drive; Teresa had never seen the Luberon before, and had insisted, again and again, round nearly every curve of the road, that I stop the car to let her out. There, in the town, in the garish midday sun, we'd stood outside the author's house, an old silk cocoon-ery in which he'd lived with his wife and daughter and son. I'm not sure what I'd expected to find there, what message, what sign, but I'd felt discouraged by the visit, somehow, though we'd laughed and joked and had a pleasant lunch there, in a crowded little place called La Terrasse. That afternoon, as we'd driven north to Beaune, where we'd planned to spend the night on our drive back to Paris, I was feeling sullen, reproachful, and had told Teresa all about Celan's final years—about his grief and madness, about the time, in his despondency, he'd attacked his wife, Gisèle, with a knife. And I'd told her about the night—Hitler's birthday—when he'd drowned himself in the Seine. He'd left a book open in his almost-empty room (by then he and Gisèle were living apart), a book by Holderin in which he'd underlined the passage: "Sometimes this genius goes dark and sinks down into the bitter well of his heart. But mostly his apocalyptic star glitters wondrously." Found also in the room was a book by Rilke, one of his favorites, a guide to French minerals, and an unfinished letter to Heidegger. He'd left the pen on his desk uncapped. I'd told her these things as we'd driven back that day, though she hadn't said a word to me, not one, had only sat there beside me, face averted, arms wrapped around her knees. Weary now, I looked out the window. The next stop was Montpellier, a city about which I knew little, except for what I'd seen before from the train. My friend Antoine had grown up there, or near there, in a town called Clapiers. It was there that he'd met his wife, Sandrine, whom I'd known briefly in Paris before she'd divorced him and taken their son back home. She was a medical illustrator, something to do with surgical equipment. I remembered one night when she'd kissed me on the lips. We were close to the city now, I could feel it: all at once there were tracts of houses again, small shopping centers, warehouses, parks, billboards, soccer fields, office blocks, and schools. The light was startling, the sky a hard and polished blue. I'd gotten out my cellphone to text Antoine, to welcome him back and to let him know when I'd return, but again was interrupted by the chiming of the little speaker above my head, and by the subsequent stirring of the woman beside me. Goodness, I must have drifted off, she exclaimed, embarrassed. Where are we, Montpellier? Yes, I told her. We've only just arrived. I watched her as she adjusted her skirt, her hair, then touched up her lipstick in the mirror on her phone. Suddenly she cocked her head at me. Her lips fluttered mutely, when, her eyes still hazy from sleep, she murmured, I had the most curious dream. I was standing on a street corner in a city somewhere. London, perhaps New York. There were people all around me, hurrying this way and that way. There were cars and delivery vans. And there was this dull clanging sound (she actually touched her ears at the recollection of it) that seemed to be coming from the ground beneath my feet, from within a large storm drain in the street, the thick black bars of which had been stamped with a beautiful flowing script, you know, like Farsi or Arabic, like the bright clear water trickling between them down the drain. She was about to speak again, when again she considered her hands. Yes, I just remembered, she exclaimed, I was holding a case! I had a dark leather case in my hands, you know, the kind for storing silverware. For some reason I was standing there with the case in my hands. Perhaps I was waiting for someone, for a taxi, a bus, though it didn't seem like it, for I was not impatient. I felt no expectation at all. Only the clanging sound—so strange and irregular—seemed to ruffle the surface of my mood, to signal my presence in time. With that she paused. She raised a hand, again I saw her lips tremble, when she smiled wanly at me. Ça alors, how strange, she whispered, a fixed, transparent look in her eyes. When I woke just now I was crying! The train had started to move again, and I followed her gaze out the window. The stone-faced embankment that bordered the track was layered with years of graffiti, a faded palimpsest of colors and styles, the words, the letters, as illegible, per-haps as stirring even, as the script in her dream. She started to speak again, then stopped abruptly, so that I turned to look at her. She had a curious expression on her face. Slowly, as if parsing the words, she said, Sometimes I wonder if I myself was to blame. To *blame*? I said. For what? For pushing him, of course. For pushing Karl onto the train tracks that day. You know, just a nudge, she said, bumping me lightly with her shoulder. The suggestion was startling and reflexively I recoiled from her touch. But you said he fell! I cried, perhaps a little too loudly, for the man across the aisle had lowered his newspaper to look at me. I didn't like where this was going. Yes, he fell, she whispered. I said that. But that's the problem: I don't remember *how*. After all no one just falls. She hesitated a moment before saying, All I recall is that it was cold and rainy that day, and that the platform was crowded, very crowded. I could feel the people pressing up behind me. I remember that. And I remember I was angry at Karl, something about the taxi ride to the station, and was trying to loosen the scarf around my neck, when suddenly the air was rent with screaming, with a hideous screeching of wheels. I struggled to speak, to reply, only to insist, But that doesn't prove anything! So you were angry with him, big deal. What makes you think you pushed him? She looked at me, amazed. What makes me think it? she repeated. Because I'd wanted to! That's what. The very thought of it had just crossed my mind. I flinched, I stammered. I could hardly believe what I was hearing and had gripped the arms of my seat to get up, when she patted my knee. True, it was only for a second, she conceded, thoughtfully, but oh how I'd hated him! I watched her as she touched her cheeks, her hair. She shook her head, I heard her chuckle, when she said, Please forgive me. I don't know what came over me. Living alone is just…is just so lonely. Some days my mind simply gets away from me. You know what I mean? Helpless, I nodded, I grinned; I didn't know what to say and fished out my cell phone, pretending I'd just received a text from someone. Unwilling to encourage her, to hear any more, I took the opportunity to finish my text to Antoine, only to be startled by his prompt reply. He was home in Paris, he told me. Tired, hungry, but home. It had been a great trip. He was only sorry I hadn't been there with him. Perhaps next time, I replied, feeling angry, resentful, for suddenly I hated my life, what little had become of it. I hated my work. What's more, I hated the fact that I was here right now on this train. Surely something had to give. I stared at my phone, I thought of the woman seated beside me, when curtly, in my ugly, make-shift Spanish, I texted my mother-in-law to tell her I'd be arriving late, due to some work on the train tracks ahead. She always offered to send a car to the station for me, though I preferred instead to hail a taxi or to walk. It wasn't far; what's more, it gave me time to get my bearings in the city, to adjust again to the pace and temper of the place. Perhaps this time I'd stop for a beer or brandy some-where, I'd get a bite to eat, for I liked Madrid by night. It was the noisy, workaday city that I dreaded, that made me cower inside most days, anxious, reluctant to leave. I pic-tured Teresa's old room, the room in which the two of us had slept, the one in which I'd sleep tonight. With its posters and notebooks, it was the room of an average teenaged girl. I used to tease her about it, about the make-up and shoes, and about the dolls and costumes in the chest by the door. Some nights, if she was feeling silly, she'd try on her old clothes for me, parading around the room to the music of one of her many cassettes. Reeking of lip gloss and perfume, she'd had me fuck her from behind. And she'd liked to read aloud to me from her journals at night, in some of which, after her father had died, she'd recorded her confusion, her grief. I'd never met him, a Frenchman named Émile who'd died in his sleep one night, in a hotel far from home. In the photographs I'd seen of him he'd looked pleasant enough, with the vague, unfounded face of someone just risen from sleep. I looked about me now. I needed to stretch my legs and to go to the bathroom, for suddenly I felt my bladder would burst. I needed to clear my head. Do you mind if I slip by you? I asked the woman seated beside me. Why, of course not, she replied, stepping into the aisle so that I could pass. I was surprised to see how short she was, the top of her head at about the level of my chin. She was still standing there, when I returned from the bathroom, chatting with a young Taiwanese couple seated just in front of us. They were on their way to Madrid for the first time and the woman from the seat beside me was recommending to them a particular restaurant on the Gran Vía, best known for its prawn brochettes. So you know Madrid well, I prompted her, once she was settled beside me again. Oh, yes, she replied. My late husband had business there, fabrics, upholstery—that sort of thing. In fact I was there just last year, to present a small Rubens to a taxi driver in Vallecas, if you can believe it, an oil sketch of the head of a Moor that was stolen by Franco before the war, only to wind up in Hamburg, in the collection of a certain high-ranking Nazi by the name of Lohse, SA-Obergruppenführer, Hinrich Lohse. Have you heard of him? No, I said, distracted by the mention of Rubens. I hadn't thought of Rubens in years, though I was pleased to think of him now, to remember Teresa's brief obsession with him and his work. At the invitation of a friend one night, and with no knowledge of the subject matter, we'd agreed, one winter, to attend a lecture on the great Flemish painter and his famous Antwerp altarpieces at the German Center for Art History near the Palais Royal. It had been years since I'd been there. The speaker, a professor from Rennes, had made no concessions to the audience that night, plunging headlong into her subject with an intensity, a technicality, that had stunned the motley assembly, barely even pausing to catch her breath as she'd described (by way of introduction, as a means of framing her concerns) the painter's vision for the famous triptych, a lecture, a narration, that soon began in earnest with a detailed, if whirlwind history of the genre of crucifixion painting itself, including (to name but the ones I remembered) the works of Grunewald, Rafael, and Michelangelo, of Titian, Bellini, Tintoretto, and Caravaggio, the ardent professor directing our attention, with the use of a laser pointer, to particular features of the images that flashed upon the screen (the line, the musculature, the expression in the eyes), before addressing her subject proper, or at least the prelude to her subject proper, by recounting for those assembled there yet another, *different* history—not so much of the painting itself, but of its critical reception over time, a history within a history, so to speak, in short a review, a survey, of the various reactions to the painting in the centuries following its completion in 1610, the professor marveling at one point (she'd actually chuckled) at the fickleness of human judgement, of taste, citing as her first example some remarks from the earliest writer to review the work, a man named Roger de Piles who'd praised the artist for achieving 'an effect of unity' and for entering so fully into his subject 'that the sight of this work has the power to touch a hardened soul', before galloping onward through the appraisals of the many critics who'd followed fast on his heels, quibblers and sustainers alike, men such as J.B. Descamps, who'd ultimately decried the paintings' 'heaviness', their lack of lightness and grace, and Sir Joshua Reynolds, who'd focused in depth, indeed to the exclusion of everything else, on the artist's use of color, which he'd admired and extolled, as well as, if not finally, the great Delacroix himself, the painter of *The Barque of Dante* and *Woman With White Socks*, who'd gone so far in his estimation of the artist as to compare the *The Raising of the Cross*—in its heroic scale and power—to Géricault's, the *Raft of the Medusa*. I remembered my surprise at Teresa's reaction to the lecture, and to the painting itself. She'd never had a moment's patience for religious subjects in art. Indeed she'd loathed them, and with an ager, a malice, she'd often vented on me, when of a dismal Sunday morning we'd wandered the rooms of the Louvre. Yet for some reason she'd been stirred by Rubens' triptych, and by the professor's critique of it, so much so that, some weeks later, we'd actually made the trip there to Belgium, to Antwerp, to see it for ourselves. I remembered it was raining that day, as we'd followed the tramlines through the tidy, narrow streets. I'd slept poorly in our small hotel, a cramped attic room, first too hot, then much too damp, too cold. And I remembered hitting my head on a beam that rose at an angle beside the bed, touching the side of my head now, as if the bruise was still there, when the woman seated beside me said, I'd never been to Vallecas, where the taxi driver lived. Apparently a Republican stronghold during the Civil War, it was bombed to smithereens by Franco's forces. The taxi driver told me so, when I met him there for lunch. He told me about his wife and daughter, both dead, and about the time he was cast as an extra in Almodóvar's film *Volver*, at least a part of which was shot there, in the neighborhood, not far from where we sat. Have you seen it, *Volver*? No? Well, neither had I, she remarked, a fact that had disappointed the poor man. Out the train window the scenery had changed again. Fields and vineyards flashed by, followed by long, lonely stretches of garrigues, punctuated here and there by ruined mills, ragged hedgerows, and old stone houses, and bisected, as in a grid, by corridors of high tension wires. Then all at once we were passing through suburbs again, through tracts of Spanish-style houses, with their palm trees and bougainvillea, in the yards of some of which I glimpsed adults and children at play. We passed a tract of open, marshy-looking land bordered by a spine of low green hills, more Spanish-style houses, crossed a river or canal, then made our way through a sprawling industrial zone, only to be dazzled, just beyond the town of Sète, by the sun-lit waters of L'Étang de Thau, a vast lagoon more than twenty kilometers long. From there it wasn't far to Narbonne. Once more I watched the woman beside me as she checked her face in the mirror on her phone, wrinkling her mouth and nose, even holding her phone at an angle above her head, so that she could examine her profile, her hair. It made me think of a story about which Antoine had once told me, a story by the author Primo Levi about an Italian mirror maker who, not content with the humdrum manufacture of conventional mirrors, as had been a family tradition for generations, had begun to experiment with their essential function and design. We were riding the métro that day, on our way to the neighborhood of Château Rouge, where he was to visit with a newly-arrived Senegalese family with whom he was working at the time, when he told me the story about the eccentric young mirror maker who'd spent his days, when he wasn't filling orders for the shop, by designing his secret mirrors. There were some that were tinted red or yellow, some with delicately blurred edges, some comprised solely of fragments and shards, and some others of streaked or milky glass. He'd made mirrors that inverted top and bottom, that reversed left and right. Working late at night in the shop, he'd made others that magnified a face or drew it far away from the viewer, as in a memory, a dream. And as a gift for his girl-friend, one day, he'd devised a wardrobe mirror from a wavy sheet of glass. Agata hadn't liked it, not at all, for if, when she'd stood before it, she'd moved even slightly, she'd found herself transformed, as by a witch's spell—her face bloated, her torso compressed, her legs as skinny as those of a heron or stork. Yet in the end such mirrors had been but gewgaws and trifles to him, for he'd had something greater in mind. Much greater. For months he'd been experimenting with different types of glass and silver plating, subjecting the materials to chemical baths, electrical charges, and different types of radiation in his effort to realize his dream: a metaphysical mirror. According to the story, a Spemet (short for specchio metafisico) defied the laws of optics, reproducing one's image as seen by the person directly facing one. One had only to ask a person (a friend, a lover, a colleague at work) to attach the small mirror to his or her forehead for the scales to drop from one's eyes, to conclude that—at least as a fixed and certain thing—one did not in fact exist. I pictured a Spemet on the forehead of the woman seated beside me and wondered what, to my amusement or horror, I'd see. She was looking for something in her handbag, mumbling, chuckling to herself, when at length, handing me a slender silver wand, she said, What do you make of it? Why, it's a yad! I cried. Yes, she replied: Bezalel, 1920's. I have the paperwork right here in my bag. Turning the pointer in the light, I admired the filigree, the finely shaped hand. They're used for reading the Torah, I declared without thinking. To keep one's fingers off the parchment. Yes, I know, she said. It was recently discovered in Bavaria, squirreled away in a drawer in the apartment of former SS commander and assassin, Klaas Carel Faber, where, following the war, he'd lived undetected until his death from kidney failure in 2012. This was his mailbox in Ingolstadt, she added, handing me a photograph from a large manila envelope in her bag. After Barcelona, I'm due to deliver the pointer to a man, a retired plumber in a town called Issigeac, not far from Bordeaux. Imagine: he had no idea he was descended from Jews! But why the photo of Faber's mailbox? I asked her. Why? Because it's part of the story, she replied simply. I looked again at the photograph, at the cleanly printed name: "K. Faber". The tag, I noticed, was tilted slightly to the left. For some reason it bothered me, as did the fact that I couldn't identify the font. Briefly I wondered if the woman seated beside me might know it, it would put my mind at ease, but it didn't seem right to ask her. Instead I said, This Faber, do you think his mailman knew who he was, what he'd done in the war? And what about his friends, his neighbors? What about the girl, the Turkish girl, who scrubbed his toilets and floors? Do you think she knew? Surprised, the woman beside me chortled in reply. *Knew?* she said. I doubt they knew anything at all, that is, anything more than the names of the magazines to which he subscribed, the particular pills he took, and the brands of toothpaste and beer he liked. Even his wife, his beloved Jacoba…how much could she have known? *Jacoba!* I nearly cried the name aloud. It was like a charm to me, for suddenly I could see her there, as she fussed about him in their tidy little kitchen, chatting, teasing him, as he leafed through the morning paper, then refilling his coffee and juice. Surely she'd loved him dearly—his hair tonic, the veins on his nose, the crumbs on his lips when he nibbled his biscuits and toast. She'd loved the smell of their evenings together, the pipe smoke, the roasted meats; she'd loved the cut of his trousers and shirts. And she'd loved the way, after lunch each day, he and Mitzi, their schnauzer, had taken a nap before the television in his favorite, pushback chair. Feeling stubborn, I said, Surely they must have known *something.* I mean, the people who saw him every day. There must have been rumors. Yes, agreed the woman beside me, I'm sure there were rumors. After all he was Dutch. Not German at all. Still, after the war, there were rumors about everyone. From what I understand, scarcely anyone escaped calumny. Yet eventually even gossip gets boring, don't you think? I didn't know; I hardly knew what to think and merely stared at the photograph in my lap, bedeviled by the crooked name card and by the ugly, intractable font. I felt a strange darkness brewing in my head, when, in the sort of voice I used for my students, I said, 'We know now that a man can read Goethe or Rilke in the evening, that he can play Bach and Schubert, and go to his day's work at Auschwitz in the morning.' Yes, she said, we know that now, don't we? Embarrassed, I explained, It was written after the war, by a man named Steiner. It's from the preface to his essays, *Language & Silence*. The book was dear to my mother, I remarked, though she hadn't always like him. The woman beside me smiled. Was she a writer, your mother? Yes, an historian, actually. She wrote a lot about the Nazis. I was going to elaborate, to tell her more, when she said, And what about you? Are you also a writer? No, I replied, at least not as such. I teach, I'm a translator. Mostly German and Austrian stuff, writers nobody seems to know! Like who? she asked. She looked intent. Well, like Ilse Aichinger, I said. Like Ilse Aichinger, Erich Arendt, and the late Swiss poet, Rainer Brambach: "Slowly the wells are running dry/The stray dogs are looking for water..." I intoned dramatically, hoping to make her smile, but she only shook her head. You're right: never heard of him, of any of them. Then what about Celan? I pressed her. Surely you've heard of Paul Celan? 'Death Fugue', 'Night Ray', 'Corona'? Right now I'm working on an English translation of his correspondence with his lover, Ingeborg Bachmann, I explained, pointing to my copy of *Malina,* which I'd stowed in the seat pocket in front of me. Or rather of *her* correspondence with *him.* Such a sad and lonely tale. He drowned himself in the Seine one night, and she, poor woman, went mad—heard voices, met with lepers, then burned herself alive in her bed. Listen to this, I said, opening up my laptop and scrolling quickly through the pages, just listen to this passage from one of her letters to Celan: "...just like you, I am absolutely in favor of remembering faithfully. In one corner of my heart, however, I have remained a romantic person; this may be to blame for my hope—a dishonest one, even if unconsciously so—of bringing back in a beautified state something I once let go for not seeming beautiful enough..." Like poetry isn't it? So nuanced, discreet. Yes, it's beautiful, agreed the woman seated beside me, when with a frown she said, I only wonder why so often such minds go so terribly wrong. We'd reached the outskirts of Perpignan, a bleached and dreary patchwork of apartment blocks, farmhouses, and rolling vineyards that soon gave way to marshlands and lagoons, and to another expanse of bright open water, when suddenly, lost in our thoughts, we were there, in the city itself, Perpinyà, at La Gare de Perpignan. Most of the station was under construction, covered in scaffolding and plywood, so that the short open section of the platform before us was crowded with travelers bound for Spain. There were businessmen and tourists, a troupe of Boy Scouts (Guides de France), and a large party of Muslim women in hijabs and tennis shoes, all talking on their cellphones beneath a large advertisement for Spanish mangoes. The fruit—one whole mango and a single juicy slice—had been arranged in a photographic still life so vivid, so enticing, I actually felt hungry again, and was tempted to get something more to eat from the café-bar, when I was overcome by a wave of sadness. For Teresa, there'd been nothing finer than fresh mangoes. I remembered the way she'd gorged herself on them, as soon as they were in season each year, eating three or four at a go, only to suck and savor the fleshy pits. I pictured her sticky hands and face, her sleeves rolled back, her eyes alight with joy. The doors of the train opened with a hiss and the passengers disembarked, bumping their way down the aisle with their bags. In what seemed like seconds they were gone, when the flow was reversed, as the passengers who'd been waiting on the platform now crowded their way onto the train. With them came new sounds and scents: Spanish, Catalan, and Arabic, as well as a heady mixture of perfumes, tobacco smoke, fast food, and perspiration, followed at length, like a cosmic exhalation, by a breath of hot dry air. Yet even after the last of the passengers had settled themselves in the empty seats around us the doors of the car remained open. From where I sat I could see part of a billboard and the large dark crown of a tree. Except for a man in uniform with a broom and dustpan, the platform was empty. I noticed that someone had left a scarf on one of the gray metal benches there, a dark tartan scarf like the one my mother had worn. She'd bought it one year, in Aberdeen, where, between conference sessions, she'd taken me to Cruden Bay to see the ruins of Slain's Castle. As a boy I'd been enchanted by the novels *Ivanhoe* and *The Lady in the Lake*, and had long dreamt of visiting Scotland, so that it had been a thrill for me to tour the windy grounds. Part of the castle's attraction for me had been the fact that the author Bram Stoker had been a frequent guest there, at the seat of the once-powerful Clan Hay. Indeed it was while he was there one winter, in that lonely castle by the sea, that he'd begun his novel, *Dracula*. I remembered my mother had had a cold while we were there, in Aberdeen, so that we'd spent much of the time reading and drinking tea in our room at the old Station Hotel, through the dark, drafty halls of which I'd occasionally wandered on my own. Our room was a funny little room with two single beds and a set of high, curtained windows that had seemed to dilute the already weak December light, making our skin and teeth look gray. My mother had given a paper while there, which, for practice, she'd read aloud to me in our room, sniffling and blowing her nose, while pacing back at forth between the soft, narrow beds. Based on the post-war deposition of a Nazi named Kurt Gerstein, an expert in 'vermin control', about whom my mother would write at length in her final book, she was to explore for her audience that day the Nazis' at first methodical, then increasingly hysterical pursuit of more efficient, more predictable, ways to kill. Appointed in January of 1942 as Head of the Department of Sanitation Techniques of the greater Hygiene Institute of the Waffen SS, Gerstein's career as a Nazi was a strange, if revealing case. The sixth of seven children of a respectable Lutheran family from Münster, he'd been quick to embrace his father's patriotism and harsh, authoritarian ways, enlisting in the ultra-nationalistic fraternity, Corps Teutonia Marburg, before joining the Nazi Party itself in 1933. Then something curious had happened. Troubled by the drunken carousing of his fellow fraternity members, he—never religious—had developed an interest in the Bible, and, in 1934, had joined the Bekennende Kirche or Confessing Church, a Christian movement vigorously opposed to the effort to unify the German Protestant churches into a single pro-Nazi force. After the war he'd described it as one of the turning points of his life. Yet there'd been another one, too, one more personal, more significant, still. It had had to do with the fate of his sister-in-law, Berta Ebeling, who'd recently died in a psychiatric hospital in Hadamar, Germany. Gerstein, having been expelled then readmitted to the Nazi Party with provisional membership in 1939, had learned one day, in the course of his work in the state sector, that Hadamar was one of six clandestine killing centers that comprised the Nazis' so-called 'Euthanasia Program', a program dedicated to the systematic murder of people with disabilities. Spurred by the belief that his sister-in-law was killed there, he'd joined the SS to learn more. What he'd discovered as a member, what ultimately he himself had participated in, had proven even crueler, more sinister. Trained in the medical corps, he'd been assigned to work in the Hygiene Institute in Berlin, where he'd quickly distinguished himself as an expert in sanitation techniques, especially regarding pest control and the maintenance of quality drinking water for combat troops. It was there, in Berlin, that he'd first heard of the Final Solution and its implementation, then well underway, eventually procuring large quantities of Zyklon-B for Auschwitz, as well as for the Aktion Reinhard killing centers at Belzec and Treblinka. My mother had quoted him at length in her final book, mostly remarks he'd made in his post-war deposition. I remembered I'd been struck by one in particular, a simple statement of fact that, for all of Gerstein's contrition, was chilling: "In this capacity I took over the entire service of disinfection, including disinfection with highly toxic gasses." Yet his story hadn't ended there. Criminal, complicit, as he'd been, he'd made a vow to himself to tell the world what he knew. One day, after having witnessed the murder of 15,000 Jews at Belzec, where he'd seen them herded from the trains, stripped naked, then packed so tightly into the gas chambers that even dead they'd stood up straight, he'd had a chance encounter with a Swedish diplomat, to whom he'd described everything in the course of their train ride to Berlin. In addition, he'd spoken secretly with officials at the Vatican (to a certain cardinal, two primates, and an elderly papal nuncio whom he'd met at a party in Mainz), as well as with a number of high-ranking members of the Dutch government-in-exile, describing for each of them, in fine, often gruesome detail, the ruthless, all but clockwork implementation of Hitler's plan, apparently none of which information had reached the Allies in time. Just before the end of the war Gerstein had surrendered himself to French authorities in Germany, by then but a shell of a man. He'd hadn't long to live. Shortly after he was transferred to the Cherche-Midi Prison in Paris, he'd hanged himself in his cell. My mother's talk had gone well that day, I remembered the dinner afterwards, the sadness, the drinks, but before I could think any more about it, about my mother and Gerstein, about Scotland and Stoker, about our damp little room at the Station Hotel, the woman seated beside me said, Here we go again! This is my favorite leg of the trip. In fact the train had begun to move, I hadn't noticed it, I'd been too distracted, and scanned the view outside. She'd always loved crossing borders, she told me; it made her feel as if she were making a run for it, that she was about to escape. It was silly, she knew. She knew that, these days, there was no escaping, nowhere to be free. Still, it's a lovely feeling, she added, in an effort to sound more cheerful, for suddenly she seemed anxious, on edge. And no wonder, I thought: she probably hadn't seen in her daughter in years. I watched her as she slipped off one of her shoes to adjust her stocking, only to ask me, Have you ever driven through the Pyrenees? No? Well, I have. When I was first married, I made the drive here with Karl. He was hardly a romantic, mind you, but the trip was one I'll never forget. One day we had to stop for a cow in the middle of the road. Imagine that! We beeped and beeped the horn but couldn't get it to move. We were somewhere north of Barcelona. I think. Night had fallen suddenly, so that, rather than push on along the winding roads, we decided to stay in a small hotel on a rocky hillside there. The toilet was nothing but a hole in the floor! Discreetly I slipped in my earbuds again, hoping she wouldn't continue her story, that she'd leave me to myself for the remainder of the trip, even turning slightly in my seat to signal my mood. The light outside had changed, the sun sinking rapidly. Between buildings, I could see in the distance the rolling outline of the mountains through which we'd soon be traveling. I too had always liked this leg of the trip. We passed some trucking depots, a long stretch of warehouses, crossed a number of dry irrigation channels, when shortly we found ourselves in the open countryside again, the landscape dotted with vineyards and old stone houses and barns, each all but concealed by thick hedgerows, and by wind-breaks of cypress and pine. Now the Pyrenees were clearly visible, capped with an icing of bright white clouds. Teresa and I had often talked of hiking there, of tracing the foot-steps of Walter Benjamin from Banyuls-sur-Mer to Portbou to stand for a spell by his grave. Yet we never had. For one reason or another, the timing had never seemed right. I was admiring the distant mountains, when sud-denly the window went dark, as we entered the first long tunnel of this stretch of the trip. In the reflection I could see the passengers seated around me, including the German, the Berliner, just behind me. With his beard and thinning hair, he was older than I expected, older than I'd deduced from his manner, his voice. His wife or girlfriend looked considerably younger than him, she was bobbing her head to some music on her large white headphones, so that briefly I wondered how they'd met, how long their relationship would last. I was listening to a rendition of Bhairavi by Ali Akbar Khan and Alla Rakha, and thinking vaguely about the couple behind me, about her breasts, her headphones, his beard, when, just as we emerged from the tunnel, I heard the woman seated beside me say, Mostly German and Swedish films. They loved them best. Confused, I looked at her. I supposed she was talking about her daughter again, about her daughter and her late husband, when as if on cue she confirmed the fact, remarking with a grimace, Ellie only ever had eyes for her daddy! They'd have gone to the movies every day if I'd have let them! She shook her head. You should have seen the way they carried on. Always laughing and teasing each other, always going on about some dreary New Wave film or another. They used to drive me crazy, the way they talked: Wenders, Herzog, Von Trotta! I wanted to blot out their names! she cried abruptly, only to chuckle to herself, smoothing out the front of her skirt. Naturally, I was happy for them, she insisted. They enjoyed each other. And why not? They were so much alike I sometimes wondered if Ellie was actually my child. Briefly she frowned. You know, she doesn't look at all like me. She has straight dark hair and a fine, beautiful voice. Even her breasts, so small, so perfect, are different than mine. Reflexively I glanced at her breasts, what little I could see of them beneath her blouse. In the moment I thought she might laugh or cry, but she did neither. Instead she said, The truth is, she hates me, everything about me! She said she hates the way I *am*. I mean, how is one to respond to that? What in the world can one say? I didn't know. All I could do was sigh and look away. The terrain had changed again: we were climbing through gently wooded hills, interrupted here and there by farmlands, and by the occasional old village nestled at the foot of a valley or spur. For some reason, I thought of the black man I'd seen outside the Gare de Lyon, after my last trip to Madrid. Drenched with rain, he was screaming—in madness or anguish, I couldn't tell. He just stood there, outside the main entrance, shrieking up at the buildings, the sky, apparently oblivious to the city around him, to the buses and taxis and people rushing by. He was neither young nor old, neither rich nor poor, but average-looking, familiar, somehow disturbingly *in-between*. He was wearing a suit, at least part of one, for I couldn't remember if he was wearing matching pants. He wasn't homeless—of that I was sure. It was the chain around his neck, a braided gold chain, that had told me so, that had suggested something else, some other explanation for his abjection, his pain. Now I looked at the woman beside me; in the late afternoon light the powder on her cheek appeared chalky, uneven, as if she'd applied it in haste. Without thinking, I said, I never really knew my mother. The woman looked up from her phone. I mean I knew her in a day-to-day sort of way, I explained. About some things I knew a lot: about the way she dressed and smoked, about the way she clipped her nails, about the way she chewed her food when she was thinking. And she was always thinking. That's mostly how I remember her—sitting in a chair or standing at a window and *thinking*. After a pause I said, It amazed me the way she could live for hours in that space behind her eyes, a space which I'd often imagined as a room of sorts, a secret chamber into which I could never find my way. It was only last year that I'd gotten a glimpse inside it, after all, when I'd read the draft of her final book. I have it right here, I exclaimed, impulsively, withdrawing it from the case by my feet. Of course, she was dead by then, the room itself gone, though I'd gotten a look inside it nonetheless, cluttered as it was with names and dates, with photographs, charts, and tables, and with a tangle of ugly German names. Yet she was there; at points in my reading

I could hear her inflections, her voice! I was about to continue, to share with the woman beside me a particular passage in the text in which I felt my mother's presence was certain, was plain, when, as if on cue, I was interrupted by the chiming of the little speaker above my head, and by the subsequent announcement—in Spanish, French, and English—that we were approaching the Spanish border, where passengers were advised to have their papers ready for inspection, a stop that once again proved little more than a formality, as soon we were moving again, winding our way south along the rocky Spanish coast. When I didn't continue, the woman seated beside me said, So what's the book about? Reflexively I riffled through the pages. For all the times I'd been asked the question, I'd never known what to reply. Often I'd said: the Nazis. It's about the Nazis. Or the Holocaust. About the men who gave the orders, pulled the levers, made the trains run on time. That was usually enough for them, whoever my interlocutors happened to be; they knitted their brows, they nodded their heads, they sipped their drinks, when we spoke of other things. Instead of responding in kind, I handed the manuscript to the woman beside me. I set it in her lap. For a moment she merely looked at it. I thought she was holding her breath, when she whispered, *The Quiet Men*, in French, then began leafing slowly through the voluminous pages, pausing here and there to consider the dedication, the epigraph, the lengthy Table of Contents, before adjusting her glasses to examine a photograph, on page 39, of three young Germans, known as 'burners', posing outside a T4 killing center in Brandenburg, where—so the caption explained—they were responsible for incinerating the corpses of murdered 'euthanasia' victims. For a time she said nothing, only stared at the photograph as if transfixed by it. She looked at it for so long I nearly spoke, only for her to finally mutter, "I hate them! I always have. I hate the way they get inside me and grow." I couldn't tell what she was referring to—the Nazis, such photographs as that one, or merely photographs in general? Still, she couldn't take her eyes off the three young men who leered back at her with the brash impunity of the dead. Patiently I waited for her to say more, to say anything, when she closed the manuscript in her lap, briefly stroking the plastic cover. She had a troubled look in her eyes. Is your mother still alive? she said. My mother? No, she's dead, I told her. She killed herself one night while I was out. The woman beside me clicked her tongue, a peculiar sound, like a clucking, clenching her hands together as if suddenly she understood something, something that had escaped her before. Do you have a picture of her? she asked. I'd like to see her face. I thought for a moment. The only one I had with me was a black and white photograph of her, aged twenty-seven or twenty-eight, dressed in evening wear and holding another woman's baby, a photograph I kept with the snapshot of Mila in the pocket of my laptop case. What made the photograph dear to me was not only my mother's beauty, her youthful grace and self-possession, but also the fact that the woman at the party whose baby she was holding was herself holding a small photograph of my mother, my sister, and me. Handing the photograph to the woman beside me, she exclaimed, Will you look at her eyes—like a cat's! And those pearls, that dress! Why, your mother is gorgeous! she said. She pointed to the toddler my mother was holding. Is that you? she said. No, I replied. It must be the other woman's baby. *That*," I said—directing her attention to the Polaroid in the other woman's hand—is me. My mother, my sister, and me. The woman beside me could hardly believe it. How extraordinary! she cried, squinting in the effort to make out our faces. I've never seen anything like it! Just then the light flickered at the window beside me. In the sky there were seagulls, and, higher up, what looked like a hawk, riding the wind against the pale blue sky. I wanted to tell her more about my mother, more about the manuscript in her lap, which I feared she'd never have the chance to read. I wanted to tell her about how my mother had suffered, about her marriage to my father, about her struggles with her colleagues, about her depression, her dejection, her grief. I wanted to stop the train right there on the track to tell her all about it, about the books and files, about the Nuremberg transcripts, about the way the Nazis—always talking—had gabbled my mother to death. Before we arrived in Barcelona, I wanted to read aloud to her certain sections of the book, which I'd marked with a pencil or pen, to share with her one part especially, a section—in appearance like a poem—that seemed to have been tacked on, added late, an appendix, an epilogue, of sorts, a grisly litter of details, events with no place of their own in time, which my mother had failed to employ in the manuscript proper, but had felt the need to include in some form, some way, a harrowing forty-one page epic of detachment, depravity, and death, in which, in no apparent order, she'd listed what remained from what she'd culled from the lengthy transcripts, a litany of facts, of depositions and affidavits, and mostly in the defendants' own words:

> *In presence of SS men, a Jewish dentist has to break all gold teeth and fillings out of mouth of German and Russian Jews before they are executed.*

> *Gas vans in D group were camouflaged as cabin trailers…*

Inmates were compelled to execute each other. In 1942 they were paid five Reichsmarks per execution, but on June 27, 1942 SS General Glucks ordered commandants of all concentration camps to reduce this honorarium to three cigarettes.

The enormous crowds of prisoners of war remained in the theater of operation, without proper care-care in the sense of prisoner of war conventions-with regard to housing, food, medical care; and many of them died on the bare floor. Epidemics broke out, and cannibalism—human beings driven by hunger devouring one another—manifested itself.

We find, as a result of our examinations and investigations, that Rudolf Hess is suffering from hysteria characterized in part by loss of memory.

By reason of a decree of 16 December 1939 by the Governor General of the occupied Polish territories, the Special Commissioner for collecting objects of art and culture was able to collect within 6 months almost all of the art objects of the country, with one exception: a series of Flemish tapestries of the Castle of Krakow.

The Führer has decided to erase Petersburg from the face of the earth.

Between March 1944 and April 1945, in Italy, at least 7,500 men, women, and children, ranging in years from infancy to extreme old age were murdered by the German soldiery at Civitella, in the Ardeatine Caves in Rome, and at other places.

Ribbentrop reflected for a moment, and then answered that this could be discussed.

They destroyed the estate and museum of Leo Tolstoy, "Yasnaya Polyana" and desecrated the grave of the great writer.

About 15 to 25 persons. The vans varied in size.

Up to 15 July 1944 the following had been scientifically inventoried: 21,903 Works of Art: 5,281 paintings, pastels, water colors, drawings; 684 miniatures, glass and enamel paintings, illuminated books and manuscripts; 583 sculptures, terra cottas, medallions, and plaques; 2,477 articles of furniture of art historical value; 583 textiles (tapestries, rugs, embroideries, Coptic textiles); 5,825 objects of decorative art (porcelains, bronzes, faience, majolica, ceramics, jewelry, coins, art objects with precious stones); 1,286 East Asiatic art works (bronzes, sculpture, porcelains, paintings, folding screens, weapons); 259 art works of antiquity (sculptures, bronzes, vases, jewelry, bowls, engraved gems, terra cottas).

Mrs. Klauber tried to inquire the reason for their actions, and was answered, 'Jews. We hate you. For 14 years we have been waiting for this, and tonight we will hang many of you.'

I shall take the liberty during the requested audience to give you, my Fuhrer, another 20 folders of pictures with the hope that this short occupation with the beautiful things of art, which are so near to your heart, will send a ray of beauty and joy into your care-laden and revered life.

The faces of the other two subjects were already pale at an early stage. Other symptoms were the same. Later on the disturbances of the motor nerves increased so much that the persons threw themselves up and down, rolled their eyes, and made aimless movements with their hands and arms. At 20 Dec. 45 last the disturbance subsided, the pupils were enlarged to the maximum, the condemned lay still. Rectal cramps and loss of urine was observed in one of them. Death occurred 121, 123, and 129 minutes after they were shot.

Amount paid over to the SS cashier: a. Camps, 6,867,251.00 zlotys; b. industrial and armament factories, 6,556,513.69 zlotys; total, 13,423,764.69 zlotys.

Very simple diet (bread and water); hard bunk; dark cell; deprivation of sleep; exhaustive drilling; also in flogging (for more than 20 strokes a doctor must be consulted).

In the Ganov camp 200,000 citizens were exterminated. The most refined methods of cruelty were employed in this extermination, such as disemboweling and the freezing of human beings in tubs of water. Mass shootings took place to the accompaniment of the music of an orchestra recruited from the persons interned.

Yes. It was perfectly clear to me that this order spelled death to millions of people. I said to Eichmann, 'God grant that our enemies never have the opportunity of doing the same to the German people,' in reply to which Eichmann told me not to be sentimental; it was an order of the Führer's and would have to be carried out.

The shooting took place by means of a measuring apparatus—the prisoner being backed towards a metrical measure with an automatic contraption releasing a bullet in his neck as soon as the moving plank determining his height touched the top of his head.

The Moor has done his duty, the Moor may go.

While the train was stopped, I'd read it all to her, page after page, insisting, if she would listen, if she would hear me, that my mother's book wasn't just a warning about things past, but about things *here* and *now*, things still to happen, to come. And, if she was willing, I'd tell her more about the writer Ingeborg Bachmann, about Bachmann, the Nazis, and Celan. It was all the same story, it was all the same thing. Now I looked out the window—hoping for what, I didn't know. The landscape, hardly different from that across the border in France, consisted mostly of irregularly shaped fields, broken here and there by patches of dark scrubby wood. The sun was just setting beyond the distant, smudge-like mountains of Puigcerdà and Andorra la Vella, where I imagined the world still covered snugly in snow. The woman seated beside me coughed suddenly, loudly, more from irritation, it seemed, than from an illness of any kind. I happened to have some cough drops and offered her one, which she readily accepted, popping the lozenge into her mouth and briefly closing her eyes.

The air on these trains is so dry, she explained, patting me on the arm in thanks. Every time I travel this way it's the same. Suddenly, with a rush of sound, we entered first one, then a series of closely spaced tunnels that signaled our approach to Girona. I was too restless to listen to music or to one of the many podcasts I enjoyed and checked my watch. From Girona it would be about a forty minutes to Barcelona Sants where I'd be able to stretch my legs and get something decent to eat. For some reason, I thought again of my sister, Colette, of my promise to return to New York, now that my father was dead. Some years ago, at her urging, I'd purchased a small apartment in Brooklyn, not far from Prospect Park, intending to move there with Teresa, who'd often dreamt of living in America, a place— to her mind—so generous, so frank, so different from Spain. Yet I'd always dreaded the prospect, for I'd never liked it there, in New York, I'd never felt at home. I'd tried to explain it to my sister, many times I'd described it—the way the city unmade me, the way it rattled my thinking, my brain. Even the drive from the airport was enough to panic me, to make me gasp and gurgle for air. The truth was I hated it there, I always had. As for the country itself, I felt nothing at all. Still, I couldn't deny the pleasure I experienced at the thought of getting to know my sister again. Some nights, when I was trying to fall asleep, I imagined myself sitting with her in her tidy kitchen, drinking coffee or tea. I'd pictured her kids, heard their squeals and shouting, felt their arms around my neck. And often, just before I fell asleep, I imagined meeting her for dinner, at some trattoria she liked, to talk about her family, her life. Perhaps she was right. Perhaps I was due for a change. Just then the woman beside me touched my arm, for we'd arrived at the station in Girona. This of all the cities in Spain, she declared to me, is where I'd like to live. I was surprised by the remark. I'd never been there before, that is, beyond the station itself, and told her so, a fact that made her frown. That's what so strange! she mused. I've never met anyone who's actually *been* here, in the city itself. If only I spoke Catalan, it's where I'd like to die. But why here? I asked. I'd scarcely ever given a thought to the place, and tried now to picture it, to picture something, anything, but no avail. As if she hadn't heard me, she said, There were Jews here, you know. They lived in a quarter called 'El Call', in the old town, on the bank of the Onyar River. That is, until Isabella came along with her 'Holy Brotherhood' and her loathsome decrees. Franco, the vicious troll, was just the icing on the cake, she added, sharply, when she admitted that the metaphor wasn't quite right. For surely there'd been nothing sweet about *him*. She leaned over me to try to get a glimpse of something familiar near the station, some landmark she knew, but there was nothing to be seen but the empty platform. And then we were off again, emerging at length into a burst of late evening sunshine, so that it felt, for a moment, as if time had been reversed, then restarted somehow. Indeed had it not been for the fact that the sun was in the west, one might have thought it was rising, for the way it quickened the prospect of the fields and highways and trees. With a cluck of pleasure, the woman beside me said, It was there, in Girona, that I first fell in love. Not love, really, but a kind of respect for myself in the company of someone else, if you know what I mean? She didn't wait for me to reply, but explained, He was not handsomer or more charming than the other men I'd known, but there was something, an air about him, a charm, it was like he had a small, strange climate all his own, an aura of sorts in which there was plenty of room for me to move, to be alone. I'd never felt that before, with anyone, the sense that I could wander off, in any direction, and never get lost. She'd said it in French, with the same strange accent. Curious, I said, So where are you from? Belgium? Luxembourg? Your accent is unfamiliar to me. Quebec, she replied, at once, and with apparent satisfaction, a place called Pont-Rouge. Then New York and Dresden. Now Paris, of course. At least a suburb of Paris, a little commune called Le

Mesnil-Saint-Denis. I'm sure you've never heard of it. It was true, I hadn't, but resisted saying so, as she seemed lost in her thoughts. In fact I was sure she'd finished talking, distracted in the moment by some thought, some memory, when she added, "It was also there in Girona that I met my dear Karl. You see, he wasn't the man I fell in love with! Certainly not. Why, you should have seen him! I disliked him at once, his scorched red face, his brusque way of speaking, his ugly, short-cut hair. He was plodding along at the end of a tour group of fellow Germans who'd stopped to ogle the view from the middle of Eiffel Bridge. He was eating chocolate ice cream or gelato, some of which had dripped down his fingers, his chin. I remember thinking he looked pathetic standing there, like a toddler in shirt sleeves and pants. And he was wearing the strangest pair of boots—like those of an alpine climber, though it was the middle of July! Even after I married him I hated those boots! At that she grinned, somewhat wistfully, I thought, though it was difficult to tell, for at once she took up her phone again, turning it anxiously in her hands. The train shuddered, the light flashed; the view outside had changed. After a brief stretch of fields, of fruit trees and vineyards, we traversed a vast stretch of forest that would have seemed remote, had it not been divided here and there by highways and roads. It was lush, darkly wooded terrain, full of deep barrancas through which one might wander, might dream. Only when we reached the outskirts of Barcelona did more houses appear, ugly, scattered settlements of them; an electrical plant with high-tension wires; and a couple of large solar arrays, the broad, angled panels of which glinted brightly in the sun. And soon we were in suburbia proper again—houses, soccer fields, swimming pools, and shops, and everywhere the tall, umbrella-shaped pines I'd only ever seen before in Rome. The little speaker crackled above my head and abruptly, after an expanse of large white warehouses, we were there, at the station, at last. The moment the train came to a halt, the woman beside me rose to her feet and collected her things. Well, this is goodbye, she said, extending a small, dry hand for me to shake. I'm pleased to have met you. I replied the same, and was about to offer to walk her out, for I was sorry we'd be parting, only to find her toddling off down the aisle. The station was deeply familiar to me, its sounds and smells, and swiftly I made my way through the milling crowds, pleased to be on my feet again. As usual, I stopped to go to the bathroom, and to wash my hands and face, before checking the information board for the next train to Madrid. Each time I passed through the busy station, I got my coffee and sandwich at the same place, at a little restaurant behind the Media Distancia ticket office, my order staunchly, invariably, the same: an iced coffee and a lightly toasted bocadillo de sobrasada. It was just as I took my place in line at the restaurant, engrossed in the thought of eating something Spanish, something good, that I saw her. There, across the crowded concourse, before a bank of orange ticket machines, was the woman from the train. Clearly at a loss, she was standing alone with her bags near the exit to Plaça de Joan Peiró. Her daughter was nowhere in sight. I watched her for a moment as she tried to get her bearings in the crowd. Map in hand, she looked older to me, even dowdy, in her soft green hat, and I was about to join her, to help her find a taxi, when I realized I'd left my Bachmann on the train.

Acknowledgements

As ever, I'd like to thank Marc Estrin and Donna Bister for their unflagging support of me and my work. I am fortunate to be working with them. I would also like to thank my friends and colleagues, David Gutierrez, Hugh Himwich, Cynde Moore, George Ovitt, Melanie Peterson, and James Wolberg, each of whom has been a source of insight and encouragement. Finally, I wish to express my love and gratitude to my family, to Linda Forcey, Margaret Nash, Franklin Nash, Suzanne Nash, Ezra Nash, Isaiah Nash, Kyra Schmoker, and my wife and partner, the incomparable Annie Nash.

Special thanks to Bishan Samaddar at Seagull Books for his permission to reprint certain letters from Wieland Hoban's *Correspondence: Ingeborg Bachman and Paul Celan*. I am grateful to both of them.

About the Author

Peter Nash is the author of the novels, *Parsimony*, *The Perfection of Things*, and *The Least of It*. He has also written a biography called *The Life and Times of Moses Jacob Ezekiel: American Sculptor, Arcadian Knight* and has co-authored a collection of essays called *Trotsky's Sink: Ninety-Eight Short Essays About Literature*. He lives in New Mexico with his wife and two sons.

Fomite

More novels from Fomite...

Joshua Amses — *During This, Our Nadir*
Joshua Amses — *Ghats*
Joshua Amses — *Raven or Crow*
Joshua Amses — *The Moment Before an Injury*
Charles Bell — *The Married Land*
Charles Bell — *The Half Gods*
Jaysinh Birjepatel — *Nothing Beside Remains*
Jaysinh Birjepatel — *The Good Muslim of Jackson Heights*
David Borofka — *The End of Good Intnetions*
David Brizer — *The Secret Doctrine of V. H. Rand*
David Brizer — *Victor Rand*
L. M Brown — *Hinterland*
Paula Closson Buck — *Summer on the Cold War Planet*
L.enny Cavallaro — *Paganini Agitato*
Dan Chodorkoff — *Loisaida*
Dan Chodorkoff — *Sugaring Down*
David Adams Cleveland — *Time's Betrayal*
Paul Cody— *Sphyxia*
Jaimee Wriston Colbert — *Vanishing Acts*
Roger Coleman — *Skywreck Afternoons*
Stephen Downes — *The Hands of Pianists*
Marc Estrin — *Hyde*
Marc Estrin — *Kafka's Roach*
Marc Estrin — *Proceedings of the Hebrew Free Burial Society*
Marc Estrin — *Speckled Vanities*
Marc Estrin — *The Annotated Nose*
Marc Estrin — *The Penseés of Alan Krieger*
Zdravka Evtimova — *Asylum for Men and Dogs*
Zdravka Evtimova — *In the Town of Joy and Peace*
Zdravka Evtimova — *Sinfonia Bulgarica*
Zdravka Evtimova — *You Can Smile on Wednesdays*
Daniel Forbes — *Derail This Train Wreck*
Peter Fortunato — *Carnevale*
Greg Guma — *Dons of Time*
Ramsey Hanhan – *Fugitive Dreams*
Richard Hawley — *The Three Lives of Jonathan Force*

Fomite

Lamar Herrin — *Father Figure*
Michael Horner — *Damage Control*
Ron Jacobs — *All the Sinners Saints*
Ron Jacobs — *Short Order Frame Up*
Ron Jacobs — *The Co-conspirator's Tale*
Scott Archer Jones — *A Rising Tide of People Swept Away*
Scott Archer Jones — *And Throw Away the Skins*
Julie Justicz — *Conch Pearl*
Julie Justicz — *Degrees of Difficulty*
Maggie Kast — *A Free Unsullied Land*
Darrell Kastin — *Shadowboxing with Bukowski*
Coleen Kearon — *#triggerwarning*
Coleen Kearon — *Feminist on Fire*
Jan English Leary — *Thicker Than Blood*
Jan English Leary — *Town and Gown*
Diane Lefer — *Confessions of a Carnivore*
Diane Lefer — *Out of Place*
Rob Lenihan — *Born Speaking Lies*
Cynthia Newberry Martin — *The Art of Her Life*
Colin McGinnis — *Roadman*
Douglas W. Milliken — *Our Shadows' Voice*
Ilan Mochari — *Zinsky the Obscure*
Peter Nash — *In the Place Where We Thought We Stood*
Peter Nash — *Parsimony*
Peter Nash — *The Least of It*
Peter Nash — *The Perfection of Things*
George Ovitt — Stillpoint
George Ovitt — Tribunal
Gregory Papadoyiannis — *The Baby Jazz*
Pelham — *The Walking Poor*
Christopher Peterson — *Madman*
Andy Potok — *My Father's Keeper*
Frederick Ramey — *Comes A Time*
Howard Rappaport — *Arnold and Igor*
Joseph Rathgeber — *Mixedbloods*
Kathryn Roberts — *Companion Plants*
Robert Rosenberg — *Isles of the Blind*
Fred Russell — *Rafi's World*

Fomite

Ron Savage — *Voyeur in Tangier*
David Schein — *The Adoption*
Charles Simpson — *Uncertain Harvest*
Lynn Sloan — *Midstream*
Lynn Sloan — *Principles of Navigation*
L.E. Smith — *The Consequence of Gesture*
L.E. Smith — *Travers' Inferno*
L.E. Smith — *Untimely RIPped*
Robert Sommer — *A Great Fullness*
Caitlin Hamilton Summie — *Geographies of the Heart*
Tom Walker — *A Day in the Life*
Susan V. Weiss —*My God, What Have We Done?*
Peter M. Wheelwright — *As It Is on Earth*
Peter M. Wheelwright — *The Door-Man*
Suzie Wizowaty — *The Return of Jason Green*

Writing a review on social media sites for readers will help the progress of independent publishing. To submit a review, go to the book page on any of the sites and follow the links for reviews. Books from independent presses rely on reader-to-reader communications.

For more information or to order any of our books, visit:
fomitepress.com/our-books.html

www.ingramcontent.com/pod-product-compliance
Lightning Source LLC
Chambersburg PA
CBHW051231210726
48290CB00003B/905